Captured!
The POW Saga of Frank Battle

A Novel by

Bob Corbin
with
Alexander Doyle

TELEMACHUS
PRESS

This book is a work of fiction. Names, characters, places and incidents are either the product of the author's imagination or are used fictitiously. Any resemblance to actual persons, living or dead, or to actual events or locales is entirely coincidental.

Captured! The POW Saga of Frank Battle

The publisher does not have any control over and does not assume any responsibility for author or third–party websites or their content.

Cover Art Design: Telemachus Press, LLC

Cover Art Illustrations:
©Copyright iStockPhoto #7146697/ChrisPole
        iStockPhoto #15898049/lukutin77

Edited by: Winslow Eliot
http://www.winsloweliot.com

Published by: Telemachus Press, LLC
http://www.telemachuspress.com

ISBN: 978-1-935670-64-3 (eBook)
ISBN: 978-1-935670-65-0 (Paperback)

2011.05.24

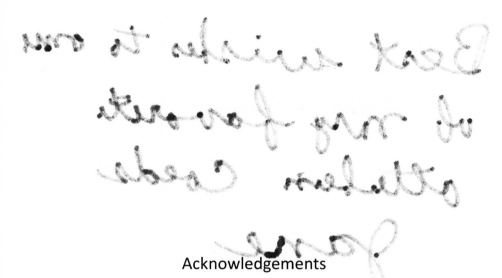

Acknowledgements

Thanks to my family and friends for all of their support and encouragement. A special thanks to Robert G. Thobaben who encouraged me to write this book and who also first documented my story in his book, *For Comrade and Country: Oral Histories of WWII Veterans*, published by McFarland and Company.

Bob Corbin, May, 2011

Best wishes to one
of my favorite
otterbein Coeds
Jane

Bob Corbin

For my Kriegie friends, Jay Drake and Dallas Smith.

Best Wishes
To my Rotary
Buddy

Bob Colbin

Prologue

Emmett Dumas waited in the hallway. He tried to push out the sensations that crowded his senses, but he wasn't too successful. The thick smell of antiseptic and cleaning fluids tugged at his nose. He knew, deep down, that those smells were hiding the smells of something more. They were hiding the death that walked the halls and the decay that nestled in the brittle bones of the men and women of this retirement home.

Emmett considered himself unique.

He was always very responsive to smell.

As a newspaper reporter, he had been sent on many a scene where there had been a murder, a suicide, or a tragic accident. It wasn't the sight of the blood or twisted metal or the way the splintered windshield glittered like diamonds in the sunlight that got to him. It was the smell.

Always the smell.

He had developed a sense for this particular smell, awareness if you will.

He smelled it now, in this lonely and deserted hallway, with it's brilliantly glaring fluorescent light and the cold echo of the footsteps that approached.

Emmett looked up from his multifunctional cell phone, where he was reading the latest mortality statistics on what he had come to know as the Greatest Generation, the World War II era. The Internet, with its relative omniscience, fed him the facts, but in his heart, he felt it as he sat in this lonely nursing home.

They were dying, thousands a day.

Someday, that number would drop to hundreds by attrition.

And then… ninety–to–fifty.

And then…tens.

And one day, the toddlers who were just learning the whole speaking thing, would completely miss out on the experience he was about to seize upon.

Why?

Because the Greatest Generation would be dead.

And the only thing left, would be their words.

What story awaited him in these halls where lives quietly faded away? For that matter, what story sat in every apartment of this nursing home? What kind of history was slipping away with the barest of whisper?

The Nurse who had been approaching interrupted his thoughts on such an impending loss.

"Mr. Dumas? He's ready to see you now."

Emmett Dumas nodded his head, stood up, with his cell phone in hand, and followed her down the hall.

The Nurse led him to a small apartment. It was nice and cozy, on the second floor of a unique high–rise. The Nurse gestured to the expensive–looking burgundy armchair. Emmett took his seat.

She went into the other room that adjoined this one, pushing a once–hearty and robust–looking man. He was balding, with large tinted glasses.

Emmett leaned forward and shook the man's hand as he extended it.

"Frank Battle, 2nd Lieutenant, POW of Stalag 13," the man's voice was a deep baritone and full of authority.

Emmett was immediately impressed.

He wasn't sure what to expect when he received a call from his wife. It was a unique situation and twist of fate, actually. She had told him about her latest visit to her grandmother, who lived on the fifth floor of this high–rise. She told him that in her visit, she had met this World War II veteran who had a fascinating story and a tremendous fear.

"Honey," he remembered her words last night as they turned in for bed, "I know you're sick of the grisly stories they put you on, day after day. You need to talk to this man. Get his story. Write about him. He just needs someone to listen. To acknowledge what he went through. You won't regret it. I promise."

Emmett agreed to visit with the veteran.

Now, as he activated the application on his cell phone that allowed him to record conversation, he felt...privileged.

"Nice to meet you, Sir," he replied. "I'm here at the request of my wife."

"Yes!" Frank brightened up, "I remember my conversation. She said she would hound you to come see me. I'm very pleased you have. I've been looking for fifty years for someone to record my story, and tell it the way it needs to be told. Seeing as how you are a writer..."

Emmett blushed, "I'm a newspaper reporter. I write the news, Sir. I can't promise I'll write a bestseller, but I'll do my best."

"That's good enough for me," replied Frank Battle.

Emmett pressed the button on his cell phone, and the recording began.

"So..." he asked, "Where do you want to start?"

Frank smiled.

"You know, Mr. Dumas, every great story I've ever read, has started with something in common. Something that we can all relate to."

"What's that?" asked Emmett.

Frank's smile somehow widened even further, "I guess you could say that it started with a woman..."

Chapter 1

Dear John and Dear Lord, I'm in a Forward Position!

Frank,
I know that you have been looking forward to my letters for some time. I've been getting all of yours. But the reason I haven't written until now is that I've been feeling like this is just not right. I'm not right. Not right for you. I'm divorced. I feel like I've got a Scarlet Letter on my forehead. I can't stand it. I just don't feel like I'm good enough for you. You deserve someone better. I know we've had a lot of great times together, and you are so very special to me. But...I just can't live like this. It's too much. So don't write to me anymore. I can't handle that. I hope you make it back safely, and you can come see me if you do. But it's over between us.
I'm sorry,
Jessica

November 25, 1944

Frank Battle sat on his bunk in his officer's quarters as he read. He chuckled to himself. Folding up Jessica's letter, he placed it in a book he had brought from the States: a fellow named Napoleon Hill had written a philosophy on leadership and success. Frank's admiration for Hill, and his subsequent dreaming, earned him the nickname 'Dreamer' from his fellow officers. Not to mention that he also talked in his sleep and kept others awake in the night. Many times he was exhausted in the morning, because the other officers had wakened him repeatedly to shut him up. But they also teased him about his "interesting" conversations with nobody in the middle of the night.

Needless to say, morning time was always an embarrassing time for Frank. He didn't know what his buddies would say to him. It was a bit unnerving too.

November 26, 1944

He placed Hill's book in his footlocker and headed out of his office, got into his Jeep, called for Frankie Redbone his driver and radio operator, and Roy, who had been recently transferred to his battery and was riding along with him to the Front to learn Frank's duty as a Forward Observer.

The 84th Division was located in northwest Germany at the time and fighting its way into the Siegfried Line. Frank, an officer who was embedded with the infantry to provide them with artillery support in their missions, was on his way to the front lines to take up his duty as a Forward Observer.

Just before he left, he received a message from Regimental Headquarters to pick up the Padre who wanted to go to the Front.

"So tell me, Padre," said Frank, as they bounced in the seats of the Jeep, "What do you believe in? Coincidence or fate?"

The Padre, from the Regimental Headquarters, a tall lanky man with graying hair, turned his head to look quizzically at Frank, "Why do you ask, my son?"

Frank shrugged, "I don't know, Padre. I just think that too many of my friends believe too much in fate."

"You mean destiny, sir?" asked Sergeant Williams sitting in the front with the driver.

"Destiny...yeah, Williams, that's maybe a better word. I don't know if I believe in destiny. Too many men I've met believe that this whole war is God's will. I don't see it. I see it as some crazy–ass Kraut's grab to have everyone kiss his ass."

The Padre smirked, "That's an interesting way to look at it, my Son. But let me ask you a question."

"Sure, Padre."

"Do you believe that you signed up of your own free will? Or did something compel you to do so?"

Frank thought for a moment.

"Well, to that, I have to say that the Pearl Harbor bombing had everything to do with me signin' up."

Padre nodded in agreement, "Okay, then can you say that you were totally free of your own volition or will to sign up? Were you completely free?"

"I guess not. Because of the influence of the bombing."

"Right! So there was an influence, no matter how small, that affected your decision."

Frank nodded. "I can agree with that."

"So if that is true, then you were not truly free, Lieutenant. You were directed, if not indirectly."

Roy, spoke up, "Some crazy–ass Jap who aligned himself with a crazy–ass Kraut who wants the whole world to kiss his ass!'"

Frank laughed. "I see your point. So you're saying that I've freely chosen to sign–up is not true. Are you saying that everything is linked to everything else?"

"Bingo!" said the Padre.

"And everything has a connection to everything else...."

Sergeant Williams turned around in his seat again, "So, Padre...there isn't anything as free will?"

"Not true free will...no...if we were truly free...I don't think we would know what to do with ourselves," he answered.

"So how does that fit with destiny, Padre?" asked Frank.

"If everything is coincidental, then nothing is planned. You can make no plans. And everything means nothing. You cannot influence anything. Destiny, Lieutenant, is part of the warp and woof of reality. Everything has a purpose. Everything has a reason. Everything happens for a reason and there is an element of good in everything that happens, because a Divine Being is watching over us."

Frank took this in, not commenting.

Suddenly the Jeep stopped in the middle of the street. Frank had been so absorbed in his conversation that he hadn't noticed they had driven all the way through Gereonsweiler. They appeared to be at the edge of the town.

"What's the problem, private?" he asked the Jeep driver.

"I'm sorry, sir," he replied, "I missed a turn. Let me back up."

The next moment, there was a mortar shell barrage. Frank heard a SPAT! behind him. He turned his head and saw a dud mortar behind him that had missed his head by three feet. His heart hammered.

He started to laugh as he felt the adrenaline blast through him.

The Padre looked scared out of his wits, which he probably was.

"Padre!" Frank exclaimed, "I believe you now!"

"What...what do you mean, my son?" he stammered.

"I wish I could drag you up to my position!"

"Why?"

"Because obviously God didn't want you dead right now! Maybe you can be my lucky charm! Wanna come?"

The Padre's eye bulged at the thought, "No, my son...I don't think I want to be your lucky charm!"

As the Jeep then began moving again, more shells fell from the sky, pummeling the town. Frank didn't seem to notice them. He was laughing too hard.

He was invincible.

As long as the Padre was with him.

"Hey Frank!" a voice pulled him out from under a restless sleep. He was covered by a blanket.

Frank blinked and shook his head.

Lieutenant Roy was cooking up something in a tin. They were in the basement of the school building that he and Roy had taken over earlier that day from "the Judge," a lieutenant, who was a lawyer from Texas.

When Frank had first met the Judge, he was cool and collected, as smooth as glass. Frank liked him. He wasn't disturbed by anything. He was as smooth in his attitude and behavior as Bing Crosby was in his best song.

Now, as Frank and Roy approached the three–story schoolhouse where the Judge was stationed, he saw another man altogether.

He was well built, and looked like he was well to do and well fed. But his eyes were pinpoints and wide, shifting constantly from side to side and ground–to–sky at the slightest gun burst ahead of the building. He ushered them into the first floor.

The three of them crouched in the basement of the building. The Judge licked his lips nervously. Frank noticed that as he pulled out a cigarette from his pouch, his hands trembled and shook violently. He could hardly hold the cigarette still for Roy to light it for him.

"Thanks..." he murmured as Roy withdrew his lighter.

"What's the situation?" asked Frank.

The Judge pulled out his map where he had been making notations on it, and began to point with a shaky finger at different positions of the German army. Frank took it all in, glancing at times to Roy, to see if he were doing the same. Roy's face was a mask of concentration.

After the Judge finished, he leaned against a wall and drew in deep drags on his cigarette. Finally, he seemed to be calming down.

Frank said, "Judge, I have to ask...what's got you so spooked?"

The Judge winced as another mortar barrage went off outside.

"You'll see, Frank. You'll see."

After the Judge left, Frank and Roy made their way up the stairs to the third floor, where the Judge had been watching the movements of the troops. The roof was devastated from mortar barrages. They stepped carefully through the debris and took up positions to begin their duty of marking German base positions. They then made their calculations for the artillery to fire on the Krauts.

Just when everything seemed to be calm, Frank and Roy heard, what he could only describe as a real–live banshee screech fill the air. Suddenly, the entire building shook as an 88mm shell ripped through the second floor below them. There was a tremendous boom and crashing noise as entire chunks of walls were obliterated and the roof on which they crouched, trembled like a drunk going through a dry spell.

Seconds later, another 88mm shell shrieked through the air, and the second floor continued to shake and rumble below them.

Frank called to Roy, "Let's get the hell outta here!"

Roy didn't argue.

As quickly as possible, crouching down as low as they could, they exited the third–floor roof and scrambled down the schoolhouse stairs to the basement. The second–story continued to bleed debris and trash. Frank and Roy returned to the classroom they had shared with the Judge and the two of them sat against the wall, wincing every time another 88mm shell slammed with terrific and horrible power into the building.

Time slowed and stretched like a thin strand of spaghetti in Frank's mind. He slipped into one of his daydreams again. He snapped out of it when Roy's hand fell on his shoulder and, wordlessly, indicated that they should go back up top.

It was only then, that Frank realized that the shelling had stopped.

The two of them made their way back up the stairs to the third floor.

They were there for ten minutes before the 88mm shells came again and they retreated back downstairs.

This went on and on...all day long.

By the time night fell, Frank noticed a slight tremble in his hands.

"I'll be damned," he murmured to himself.

That night, Frank and Roy were in the basement of the Command Post with Captain Walsh, giving him details on German movements and positions. An infantryman came in and reported that they had just captured a pillbox fifty yards in front of the lines. Frank was excited. A pillbox was a concrete, dug–in guard post, sometimes equipped with loopholes through which weapons could be fired. As soon as Captain Walsh dismissed the infantryman, Frank could hardly contain himself.

"Sir!"

"Yes, Battle?"

"You know, I could do a much better job if I was in that pillbox, Sir."

Roy didn't say anything; he just looked back and forth between Battle and Captain Walsh.

"I don't think so, Battle. It's too risky."

"But sir, if I were in that pillbox, nothing could touch me! I'd be totally protected!"

Captain Walsh paused.

Frank pressed the advantage, "Captain...we *need* someone in that box! Roy and I need someplace that is totally covered! We're completely exposed on that roof! If we were in that pillbox..."

Frank, seeing that the Captain was possibly reconsidering, closed his mouth, thinking that if he pressed too hard, he'd get shut out.

Captain Walsh returned to look at he maps they had and marked where the pillbox was. Battle could barely contain himself, but he did. In his mind, he was thinking of how safe he would be from the Krauts.

Finally, after a long time, Captain Walsh turned back to Frank and Roy.

"Okay, Battle, you convinced me. You and Roy will head to the pillbox at 0600 tomorrow morning."

Frank and Roy saluted him simultaneously, "*Sir*!"

"Dismissed. Now go get some chow."

Frank and Roy left with grins on their faces.

Chapter 2
Pillbox

At 0600 the next morning, Frank met Lieutenant Roy with a runner to take them to the captured pillbox. All night long, Frank had entertained dreams of being safe from the 88mm shells that had honeycombed the school where he had been positioned. From a pillbox, he could work in safety. After spending a day running up and down the stairs of a three–story school building, he now understood clearly why the Judge was so shaken.

His hands had stopped shaking, and he wanted it to stay that way.

The pillbox would give him that.

The three men set off on foot into the midst of the German town.

The morning fog was thicker than pea soup, but that was fine by Frank. The thicker the fog, the more their movements would be untrace-able by the enemies' own Forward Observers. The last thing he wanted was to be pinned down and captured by the Krauts when he was so close to safety.

Frank finally recognized the tune Roy was humming. It was Sinatra's "I've got the world on a string."

Frank smiled to himself.

Once he was in that pillbox, he would join Roy in humming the tune.

Their runner turned to Frank after a couple of blocks into their jour-ney, "LT, there's a sniper down this way…can we take another route?"

Frank wasn't particularly eager to be another notch on a sniper's belt. He nodded his head, "Go ahead. Just get us there, I'm not out here taking in the town like some googly–eyed tourist. Got me?"

The runner, a private, saluted, "Yes, sir!"

Frank returned the salute and the runner turned to the left at the next intersection. Frank and Roy followed behind, confident that they were well on the way to safety. Roy continued to hum Sinatra.

Frank, feeling somewhat secure from the sniper, allowed his thoughts to take him back a couple of years.

It was 1942, and Frank was with his girlfriend, Maryann. There was a Sinatra concert at the local concert hall. His friend Mickey Jones had managed to somehow gain access to the concert hall while Ole Blue Eyes was rehearsing for that night. Mickey and his girl, Rhonda, had encouraged Frank and Maryann to join them for a little B & E. Mickey knew a friend who had a key to one of the stage doors. Mickey had borrowed the key from his friend.

That day, Mickey, Rhonda, Frank, and Maryann used the key to enter the concert hall. Not wanting to get caught and kicked out (or arrested) the four quickly and quietly made their way to the top of one of balconies. There, they sat on the floor for the next two hours, listening to Sinatra croon through hits like "Witchcraft," "I've got you under my skin," and "Nice and easy."

Frank tapped his foot and sank into Blue Eyes' voice, forgetting everything.

A couple of times, Mickey almost gave them away, but Rhonda shushed him when he tried to sing along with Sinatra. Frank playfully punched him in the side when he got just a "little" too loud. Mickey was a goof who always pushed the envelope.

Finally, after a couple of hours, it seemed that Sinatra and the band had decided to take a break. So instead of just sitting there like frogs on a log, the four of them decided to make their way back to the exit. As they turned down the stairway from the balcony, a lone figure turned the corner, and the four of them found themselves face–to–face with Ole Blue Eyes himself.

Frank was slightly taller than the singer, but he didn't notice that. What he noticed was Sinatra's eyes. They weren't blue in this corridor. They were dark. Dark and deep. Frank found himself captured by the man's gaze.

The singer looked surprised for just one solitary moment before a smirk broke out on his face.

"Well...well...look at this!" his voice contained a hint of mirth, "I got myself some fans!"

Frank glanced at Maryann, who could only stare and gape like a scarecrow. Mickey swallowed, and Rhonda squeaked.

"Uh, sir," started Mickey, "Please don't call the cops on us! We just..."

Frank Sinatra waved his hand, to silence Mickey, "Don't worry boy! I'm good to my fans! Why don't you four come to the front row? My treat!"

Frank was overwhelmed.

Maryann and Rhonda squeaked simultaneously.

Mickey just worked his mouth silently, unable to find his voice.

When nobody moved, Sinatra got a serious look on his face.

"Boo!" he burst out suddenly.

All four of them jumped, and Sinatra laughed a deep booming laugh.

"Come on you guys! Follow me!"

With that, Ole Blue Eyes treated the four friends to a private and amazing show. Before long, the band came back, and joined the Chairman. The four of them sat in their seats, completely overwhelmed.

It was the gunfire that brought Frank out of his daydream. He slammed himself against the nearest wall. Roy joined him a mere moment later. Frank shook his head, trying to clear away his memories that threatened to crowd out his awareness of his present situation. The runner was across the street, crouched within a doorway, rifle in hands. He peered out down the street.

The gunfire shattered the silence of the morning fog, crisp and staccato.

But it wasn't anywhere close to them. Now that they heard it again, it sounded like the shooting was happening about three streets over from them.

We need to get to that pillbox!

Again, Frank allowed his thoughts of safety to drive him forward. The three of them waited until the gunfire died down. Finally, after what seemed to be forever, Frank motioned for them to move out and press forward.

The runner took point, and Frank and Roy followed.

The streets were deserted, and as the morning wore on, gunfire began to break out all over. Short bursts to the left and ahead, right and behind, two streets to right, one street behind them. The three men pressed on, determined to reach the Pillbox.

Then, after what seemed a long stretch, the gunfire ceased.

The runner stopped.

"What is it, private?" asked Frank.

"Uh, sir..." he paused, glancing around, "I've lost my bearings.... can you wait here? Let me go over that hill there." He pointed to a small rise about a hundred yards ahead.

Frank looked at Roy, who nodded his agreement.

"Go ahead, private."

The private saluted and then took off.

Frank and Roy leaned against a low fountain. They were sitting in the middle of a square where several streets intersected. The water trickled pleasantly, and Frank almost found himself drifting into another daydream.

Once again, it was the gunfire that broke that direction of his thoughts.

"Aw dammit!" cussed Roy. "That damn fool just gave us away and got himself dead!"

Frank said nothing, just sat crouched with his rifle, eyes scanning the horizon, waiting for the appearance of the Krauts. In his mind's eye, he could see them pouring over the hill with guns blazing. Despite the November cold, he began to sweat.

It didn't take long for the gunfire to die.

Frank and Roy adjusted their grips on their rifles, and waited.

Waited for the Krauts.

Time stretched as Frank tried to calm himself.

Suddenly, a lone figure appeared over the hill.

He waved his arms.

It was the private.

"All clear, sir! This way! I'm sure!"

Frank exhaled violently, not realizing that he had been holding his breath. He glanced at Roy, whose expression mirrored his feelings of unease.

"Let's get to that damn pillbox!" mumbled Roy.

Frank nodded wordlessly and rose from his crouched position.

Meeting the private at the top of the hill, he addressed Frank, "Sir, it's just a couple of streets ahead! I'm sure of that!"

Frank nodded, "Lead on, private."

The three of them moved through the morning fog silently. Roy had given up his humming.

As they crossed the second intersection, they saw a defensive post occupied by some soldiers who appeared to be checking their guns.

As they passed the post, Roy waved to them, "Morning boys!"

They just looked up at them and watched them walk past.

Frank, Roy, and the private walked for about another hundred yards before a voice rang out in the morning fog, "Hansup! Coom out!"

Instantly, Frank thought of the article he had read in the Stars and Stripes just a few days before. It had said that some Germans were surrendering, but the only English they knew was, "Hansup! Coom out!"

Well...I'll be...They want to surrender!

As a group of about three figures materialized out of the fog in front of them, Frank aimed his gun at the speaker as he repeated his statement.

"Hansup! Coom out!"

Before he could get the next words out of his mouth, offering the man a chance to relinquish his weapon, the German fired at him. Frank felt something rip through his left arm jacket. He looked down and saw where a bullet had just ripped through his sleeve, barely missing his elbow.

When he looked back up, he saw that the Germans had their guns trained on them. Then he heard footsteps from behind them. Glancing behind, he saw the soldiers that Roy had just waved and said something to approaching them with weapons raised. It was then that he saw the uniforms they wore were not Uncle Sam's.

Roy realized this at the same moment.

"Aw...dammit!"

The three of them raised their hands in the air.

Chapter 3
Captured

Frank kept his hands raised behind his head as the German soldiers took his weapon and ammunition away from him. He kept his eyes on the Germans' guns that were trained on him. There was no telling what would happen now.

I could try to make a run for it if...

A glance behind them showed the hill they had come over was only a short sprint away.

It was only a short sprint.

In his mind, Frank saw himself breaking away, running back the way they had come.

His feet pounded the concrete road as his lungs filled with air. The German shouts chased him.

"Run, Frank!" Roy shouted. "Run!"

"Go! Go! Go!" Frank urged himself on, his steps consuming the yards. His breath exploded out of his mouth, the blood pounding in his ears.

Though his breath and heartbeat crowded out the world, he dimly heard the click of the burp guns behind him. He heard the German command shouted out by the officer.

There was a whizzing sound around him as bullets strafed the ground beside him.

Frank kept running.

"Stoppen! Stoppen Amerikaner!" German commands chased after him with their thick accents.

Frank kept running.

He heard the German CO call out something after him.

Frank didn't know what that was, but instinctively, he knew it was bad. When the bullets ripped through him, cutting his legs out from under him, exploding his lungs, stomach, and heart as they blasted through him. Blood filled his mouth as he fell, pain overwhelming him.

Frank opened his eyes to find a German staring at him, his burp gun trained tightly on him.

It's not worth it.

The German standing before him appeared to be his age, maybe a year or two younger. His blond hair was a shock of yellow in contrast to his ice–colored blue eyes.

This guy is a kid like me.

He glanced at the other soldiers that had their eyes on them. They, too, were young. If he had been a German, they could have been his classmates. They could have been his best friends. But that uniform, that swastika, that burp gun, said differently.

Another soldier stripped Frank of his backpack and began rummaging through it. They took his k rations and other supplies that it carried. The Germans began to pass out his supplies amongst themselves. Frank glanced at Roy as he began to curse under his breath. His backpack was being stripped of its contents as well. Roy returned his look with an expression on his face that said, "Well, ain't this a fine mess!"

The private stood on the other side of Roy, his eyes full of terror.

"Take it easy, private," said Frank, "don't make trouble and you'll be fine."

"*Schweigen!*"

The barrel of a burp gun filled his vision as the speaker stepped up to Frank.

"*Schweigen!*"

Frank closed his mouth and stared at the barrel of the gun.

It mesmerized Frank.

The promise of certain death hung between Frank and the soldier. Just the slightest word or movement would bring an end to it all.

"*Scheigen!*" The soldier ordered him.

A translation wasn't needed. They didn't want him talking. That was clear.

After they had completely looted his and Roy's backpack, the German officer, who appeared to be in charge of the soldiers who surrounded them, said, *"Nehmen sie an die Leitstelle."*

The blond soldier in front of Frank nodded his head in acknowledgement of his CO's order. With a gesture, he barked, *"Bewegen!"*

Frank didn't know German, but he could guess what that meant. He turned slowly toward the direction that the soldier pointed with his gun. Roy and the private followed behind him.

With two soldiers to a prisoner, they followed the soldiers who led them. With a steady pace, they moved deeper into German–held territory. They walked several blocks turning several times both left and right, to a point where Frank lost all sense of direction. He tried to keep a frame of reference in his head, but it was hopeless after a while.

In the distance behind them, periodic strains of gunfire and shelling called after Frank and his fellow captives. He was now beyond that front line. He wondered if he would ever see his CO again. If he would ever see his Mom and Dad again. The way that they had blundered right into this mess, he was pretty certain, ensured that no one on his side would know what happened to him.

The thought that his mother wouldn't know what happened to him was unbearable to Frank.

"Stoppen!" the German command snapped Frank out of his reverie. He could guess what that word meant.

They were now in front of a bunker. The soldiers motioned with their burp guns for the three of them to enter into the structure. As they entered, Frank noted the sparseness of the bunker, not unlike ones he had already seen that the Allies had captured. It was, of course, stocked with ammunition, food stocks, and radio equipment. A row of cots lined one end of the building. Along the walls were posters of Germany in all her glory.

Frank examined posters of Hitler standing in salute to the troops. Another poster had, Frank assumed, a famous German actress, waving a Nazi Swastika flag, with the words, *"Für das Vaterland!"* in bold black underneath her picture. The rest of the wall decorations consisted of the Nazi flags and other propaganda.

Three chairs were brought out, and the German officer who had led their group to the bunker stepped in front of them, motioning them to sit. They did, and he turned his back to them, rummaging through a box that contained some papers. When he turned around again, he passed out to each of them a copy of the same document. Frank took the document and examined it.

The top half of the page was a colored drawing. It was of a woman, dark haired and wearing lingerie that bordered on indecency, embracing a dark figure wearing a black cloak and shrouded in darkness. Below the picture, Frank saw the writing was in English.

It read:

Sally Smith has had a long day at the bomber factory, building planes for the war effort. She tried to, once again, remind herself why she was doing this. It was for Billy, her husband, now overseas fighting the Germans. The last she heard from him was 3 months ago. His letters stopped coming. Now, her life consists of working in the factory, driving home, checking the mailbox for letters, and cooking a lonely dinner for one.

Tonight, however, she will be going out to dinner with her supervisor, Donald, who has noticed her in his daily inspection of the factory and taken time out to speak to her personally. Although she is married to Billy, there was something about her supervisor that excited her. Perhaps it is the fact that she is so lonely without Billy. Perhaps she is tired of one–person dinners and empty mailboxes.

The doorbell rings, and Sally calls out, "It's open! Come on in!"

Donald, her supervisor, enters the house. Sally is in her bedroom, changing clothes. She calls out to him, "Go ahead and fix yourself something to drink!"

Donald likes this idea, and he goes to the liquor cabinet where he pours himself some American whiskey. After filling his glass, Donald casually strolls toward the hallway, where he sees that Sally's bedroom door is open.

Sally is in the midst of changing her clothes when she looks up and sees Donald standing in the doorway. Instead of acting with surprise and embarrassment, Sally smiles at Donald. Donald smiles back and sets his American whiskey on the dresser table as he enters the bedroom and into Sally's embrace. Sally doesn't think of Billy as she enfolds Donald into her arms. She is just thinking of how she doesn't feel alone anymore.

This could be your wife.

This could be your sister.

This could be your mother.

What they don't know, is that they are embracing your death. They are moving on with their lives.

What will you do?

Frank looked again at the dark figure that was embracing Sally. He then noticed that the figure had skeletal hands. It was Death she was embracing.

Franks thoughts turned back to the moment he opened the letter from his girlfriend just a couple of days before. He remembered clearly what she had written. There was no mistaking it or misinterpreting what she meant.

The next moment, Frank suddenly felt a laugh bubble up from inside of him. It came so quickly he couldn't suppress it. The expression on the German officer's face was one of puzzlement and surprise as Frank started to laugh, and not just small laugh. This was, what his father called a gut buster of a laugh.

Roy looked at him with a confused expression on his face. The private mirrored that look.

Frank didn't care.

The laughter that boiled out of him continued for quite a few moments.

The lunacy of events was starting to catch up with him. When he looked back down at the paper he held in his hands, the one that was supposed to demoralize and drive him to despair, his laughter doubled to the point where he almost had tears come to his eyes.

If only they knew!

Chapter 4
Interrogation

"Oh God Almighty! Kill me now!"

It was the middle of the night, and a new prisoner was brought in. "Please, Mary! Mother of God! Take me now!" he pleaded.

He threw himself on a bunk, hardly able to stand, and went on screaming, praying for his mother, for God, for Jesus Christ to take away the pain. His feet were black from frostbite.

They didn't know what the man's name was, but Frank thought of him as the Damned One. He closed his eyes and tried to dream himself out of this prison in which he found himself. Roy's voice intruded on his dream.

"Hey, soldier."

Roy was kneeling at the Damned One's bunk. He was a young man of about 22 years old, Frank judged. His own age.

The Damned One opened his eyes that had been squeezed tight. His breath was coming in hitches and gasps. The pain must have been unbearable.

"Yeah?" the Damned One gasped.

"That's yeah...sir!" corrected Roy. He held out his dog tags showing his rank. "You suffering from frostbite?"

The Damned One somehow managed a weak salute, "Sir?"

"What's your name, soldier?"

"Hanks, sir."

"What happened to you, Hanks?"

Hanks' answer came between desperate gasps and groans, "I was with patrol of three people who decided to take a machine–gun nest. We were in twenty–five feet of the nest when we got pinned down. It was the middle of a snowstorm. Everyone died but me. Even though I was alive, I got a severe case of frostbite in both of my feet. For two nights, I lay there, not moving, in front of the nest. They found me and brought me here."

Roy glanced back at Frank; the look on his face spoke volumes to Frank. *This boy needs to be put down like a lame horse.*

Frank only nodded in silent agreement, but he was unwilling to do it.

The rest of the night, Americans and their German guards endured Hank's agonizing cries of pain and request for death. It was a wonder it hadn't already happened.

Somehow, Frank managed to slip into a semi–sleep state, because the next morning, he realized that Hanks was gone. They had moved him to another room, perhaps for treatment.

He looked around their confinement quarters. It was a room about twenty feet long by ten feet wide, crammed with German bunks covered with thin blankets and lumpy pillows. Two Germans who sat at a small table, playing cards, guarded the only door to the quarters. Well, they looked like they were playing cards, but they were obviously more focused on their prisoners' movements than anything else. Frank, from his vantage point, could tell that the one Kraut had a winning hand several times, but he didn't seem to play it right. Instead of winning the hand, he would stop, look at his charges, and then make notes in a small leather notebook. Obviously, these notes would be passed onto their interrogators when they came.

Frank, not wanting to be an easy mark for the German officer who would question him, decided to play it cool. After he realized that the Germans were taking notes on everyone, he resigned himself to as little activity as possible. He lay on his bunk and pretended to sleep, occasionally opening one eye to study the German's card playing skills. Which were either really poor, or just a feint. The way the man took notes, though, made Frank think that he was a pretty sharp guy. His companion, didn't seem to notice when he took the notes, he just kept playing like nothing was wrong or interrupting their game.

Frank guessed that they were being held at the Division Headquarters for this region. After his experience in the bunker with the hilarious attempt to demoralize them, he, Roy, and the private had been driven to a large building that was heavily fortified and decorated with heavy artillery. The ride over would have been uneventful, if it weren't for the fact that they had experienced another of what Frank was now calling a "Padre Moment."

As they were traveling, they stopped at an intersection, preparing to turn right, when a shell landed right behind the jeep. It didn't go off. Frank and Roy just looked at each other, with an unspoken thankfulness on their faces. The jeep continued on, and Frank felt a sensation of being watched come over him. This wasn't a physical sensation of a type where he could feel someone's eyes on him. No, this was different. It was a different set of eyes, he was coming to believe, that watched over him, a set of eyes that belonged to a higher dimension of reality. Whether that was proof of God or not, he wasn't willing to say yet. But there was something there...something.

When they arrived, Frank and Roy were separated from the private, and he wasn't sure what happened to the man.

Now the door to the room opened up, and the two men playing cards sprang to their feet. A German officer, a lieutenant, Frank guessed, walked through with a pair of armed German soldiers. This man was dark–haired, with a thin, long face, and dark eyes. He had a thin frame but when he walked, there was an economy of movement. He looked around the room until his eyes rested on Frank, and then he leaned down and whispered something to the guard, his eyes still on Frank. As Frank sat there, he felt the man's eyes mark him as a predator would mark their prey.

The note–taker handed him the leather notebook. The German walked over to Frank and stood in front of his bunk.

"American," Frank was shocked to hear very clear and precise King's English come out of the German's mouth, "Come with me."

"Well, I guess I don't have a choice, do I?" Frank mumbled as he rose from his bunk.

"No...you do not have the luxury of choice anymore," the lieutenant replied without any hint of a German accent. "For you, American, the war is over."

Frank nodded in agreement and flanked by the German soldiers, left the confinement quarters. They only walked up a flight of stairs to the second floor and into an office decorated with Nazi flags, and what appeared to be commendations and awards, medals, and plaques. There was a single chair in front of the desk, and Frank took his seat. The lieutenant walked around the desk and took his seat.

"Leave us," he ordered, and the German escorts disappeared through the doorway.

The German leaned back in his chair, and put his hands together in a thoughtful steeple of fingertips. He looked at Frank for a long time, weighing him.

Frank, not wanting to give into the scrutiny, studied the German's desk. It was essentially bare, with the exception of a photo frame, some file folders, and a notebook and pen. Frank supposed that the photo was of the officer's sweetheart.

"So what is your name?"

"Name is Frank Battle. Rank 2nd Lieutenant."

"Ah...a fellow officer. Your dog tags?" He held out his hand expectantly.

Frank laid them in the man's outstretched hand. He examined them for a second, wrote something in the notebook, and then handed them back to Frank. Frank slipped them back around his neck.

"And you are?" Frank asked, not wanting to be at a disadvantage.

"I am Major Alexander Stieg, SS."

SS? Oh my God! What have I gotten into?

But it made sense. Who else would be most appropriate and well suited for interrogations? The most devious, crafty, and ruthless bastards in the whole of the Nazi nation, that's who. Frank managed to keep his composure and poker face.

"You may think of resisting my questions, but you will quickly discover that we will overcome any defense you may have."

Frank couldn't conceal a burst of incredulous laughter, "Alexander, I don't think that you guys are in much of a position to overcome anything! We're on your front door!"

"That means nothing," he said dismissively.

"So where did you learn the King's English?"

"A wonderful question!" Stieg cried, "I was a purser on the *Queen's Garden*, which sailed between Liverpool and South America. I so love practicing my English skills! I find the English language very interesting...not as colorful as my own, of course, but it has merit, I believe, in its own right. Perhaps the Fuehrer will allow the language to stay after we have overcome you."

Frank watched the Major closely. His eyes never seemed to blink.

"I'd say 'pleased to meet you', if it weren't for the fact that I'm your prisoner and you my captor."

"A smart mouth...this one," said Stieg, his disapproval and condemnation lowering the already cool winter temperature of the room.

The more that he watched this man, the more he reminded Frank of a wolf. He even looked like a wolf, a predator to be avoided at all costs.

"I'll keep that in mind," Frank replied, but feeling the weight of SS officer's eyes on him.

"And your duties include?" Stieg had his pen poised to write.

Frank shifted in his chair.

"If you want to talk about my duties, I have to respectfully decline to comment upon any military subject you wish to discuss."

Stieg frowned, and his expression held within it, a sense of disappointment and something else. Frank wondered what that was.

"I see..." Stieg said resignedly.

"However," Frank spoke up, with a hint of sarcasm, "If you want to discuss your mother's pie–cooking skills or my mother's ability to make a damn good roast beef sandwich, I'm willing to talk all day about that!" Frank barely kept his grin from spreading across his entire face.

Major Stieg muttered something under his breath, and Frank strained to hear what it was.

"Yes," he sighed to himself, "he is a smart–ass."

Frank couldn't prevent the feeling of accomplishment that washed over him. They would get nothing from him.

"Very well..." Stieg said, "I suppose we will have to try again later."

Stieg stood up and walked around the desk, opened the door to the office and beckoned the uniformed escorts inside.

"Take him back to his quarters."

Frank stood and followed the soldiers out of the office. It wasn't until the door closed behind him that he felt a slight relief and relaxation between his shoulders. The man who resembled a wolf couldn't look at him anymore.

The next day, Stieg returned, and this time, chose Roy as his subject. Frank did as little as possible, waiting until Roy was brought back. When he did, Frank questioned him about the interrogation. Roy made it clear that Stieg made as much headway with him as he did with Frank. Frank took a delight in being able to frustrate the SS officer.

Frank closed his eyes, and in the darkness, saw Major Stieg staring back at him.

Chapter 5
Who's on First?

On the third day, it was soon after waking that Stieg arrived and beckoned to Frank. Without resistance, Frank followed the guards out the door and back upstairs to the Major's office.

As he sat down in the chair, he noticed that there were some new documents on Stieg's desk. He recognized them as the maps and documents that he and Roy had carried as they had made that fateful trip into German territory just a few days ago. Stieg sat down and began to peruse through the documents, without saying much. Then finally, he looked up at Frank and folded his hands.

He was silent for a moment, seeming to weigh his next words. Then he sipped from a steaming cup of what looked like tea.

The thought of tea was appealing to Frank, even though he was not much of a tea drinker. Anything would be an improvement over the bare meals they fed them in their confinement. He found himself eying the cup of tea a little too long. Stieg noticed this.

"Would you like some?" he offered, turning to the hot plate that sat on a filing cabinet beside his desk. He poured the hot tea into a cup that had been resting next to the pot. With an unusual degree of care and etiquette he set the cup in front of Frank and then leaned back in his chair as far as he could, hands folded behind his head.

Frank looked at the tea on the desk before him, realizing what was happening. He's trying to make me as comfortable as possible. This is a trap. *If I drink that tea, I'm accepting his hospitality, but it also means I'm obligated to him. I'll owe him. I can't do that.*

Frank raised his eyes to look at Stieg's dark ones. They reminded him of Sinatra's.

I'm sitting across from Ol' Blue Eyes! He barely stifled a smirk.

"What is it?" asked Stieg in the kindest voice possible, "Think of something funny?"

Frank allowed himself a little grin and chuckle, "Yeah, you could say that."

"Good! I love a good laugh! Let's hear it!"

Frank looked down for a second to gather his words.

"I was just thinking how I'm sitting across from Ol' Blue Eyes himself!"

"Ah! Sinatra!" exclaimed Stieg, "I enjoy that crooning voice of his!"

Frank nodded, "Yeah, so do I. I met him once, you know."

"Did you now?"

Frank nodded, "I snuck into a concert hall with some friends one time where he was preparing for a show. We met him up close and personal. He even gave us a private show."

"Did he now? How excellent!" Stieg clapped his hands together in amusement, "How delightful! What a wonderful tale! Now tell me what you know about the placement of artillery along your territory."

Suddenly, his face shifted within a heartbeat, from one of a kind and generous man, to one of stone and hardness. The steel in his eyes, his deep dark eyes, sparkled with the sharpness of a razor.

Frank didn't miss a beat. His eyes dropped to the still–untouched tea sitting before him. "You know I can't do that, Stieg. I won't do that. Let's talk about something else."

Stieg sighed loudly.

"Battle, Battle, Battle. Do you realize that I can send you to the Western Front where the POWs live in nightly terror from the American bombers? If you don't play nice, I'll be forced to not be very accommodating to you."

"Well...Stieg, if you want to be accommodating to me and my buddy, let us go. That's as accommodating as you can get!"

"Ah! The smart–ass speaks!" he declared triumphantly.

Battle smirked, "Hey, I come by it naturally. What can I say?"

Stieg leaned forward, "Tell me what the differences are between the British and American battalion armaments!"

Frank couldn't suppress the laughter that burst out of him.

"You really are desperate aren't you, Stieg?"

Stieg's face hardened.

"Get out!" he hissed.

Frank stood up, and walked to the door. Stieg called out to the guards in the hallway. A second later, the door opened and Frank was escorted back to the confinement quarters.

Day Four of their confinement proved to be their last day in the Command Post. Roy returned from another meeting with Stieg. Shortly after, Stieg returned with four escort guards and summoned the two of them.

Stieg led them to a German staff car where the four guards surrounded them as they sat in their appointed places. The guards' faces were blank and expressionless. Stieg sat in front with the driver.

Roy and Frank said nothing to each other, but the question hung in the air between them.

Where were they going?

Execution?

POW camp?

More interrogations?

They traveled for about twenty minutes before stopping. Above them towered a massive building that was even more guarded and fortified than the Command Post they left.

"Where are we?" Frank asked, looking around.

"Regional Headquarters Artillery for Western Front," Stieg answered, nonchalantly.

With that, Stieg gestured, and the four guards escorted Frank and Roy into the building. They didn't walk far before they were taken into a large conference room. On one wall was a huge map of the Western Front of the German defense lines. On a massive desk were a series of smaller maps, documents, and black and white photographs. The room was lined with chairs, and they were directed at gunpoint to sit in chairs against the wall.

Frank couldn't take his eyes off the giant wall map. On it were detailed positions of what appeared to be every Allied and German division and military position.

If we could get that map to our commanders, it could change everything.

Frank noticed a very luxurious staff car pull up out front. A German general who was almost beautiful in his uniform that was covered with medals and decorations got out. He was the most elegant officer Frank had ever seen.

This general came through the door and stood beside Stieg, examining some documents on the desk. When he looked up, he looked straight at Frank, his eyes penetrating and sharp. There was a look on the man's face that Frank didn't like. It went beyond a derision of him as an enemy. No, that look went deeper than that.

"Who is that?" whispered Roy.

Frank could only shake his head slowly, imperceptibly. Any real communication between the two of them would be observed and punished. Still...

"Roy..." Frank murmured as low as he could.

"Yeah?"

"Follow my lead when it's time."

"Sure thing."

Fortuitously, the next moment, Stieg sent the only guard with a burp gun into the hallway. Then it was just Stieg, a nameless lieutenant, and the general. Frank eyed the man's sidearm.

The general walked around the desk and eyed Frank and Roy closely. As he passed by Roy and himself, Frank smelled a thick cologne fill the air. He almost choked, it was so strong. The man appeared to Frank as fine an example of a spit–and–polish a General as he had ever seen. His clothes were crisp and pressed. His boots were spotless and polished. His hair was groomed and perfectly cut, perhaps even that morning.

Stieg snarled at them, "You should come to attention in the presence of General Rhinestadt!"

Frank looked at Roy, who shrugged his shoulders, as if to say, 'He's not my general.'

Frank returned a defiant look at Stieg, who was quickly crossing the room toward them. But a word from the general stopped him cold. Stieg turned and saluted Rhinestadt. The general walked around the desk and took a seat. He cast his gaze upon Frank and Roy and motioned for them to come forward.

Stieg spoke up, "The general would like to have a word with you both. Approach the desk."

Frank and Roy rose from their chairs and walked slowly toward the desk. Stieg closed in on Frank, just a step behind him. Frank could feel the man's breath on his neck if he focused hard enough. Frank began examining everything in the room, taking it all in at once.

The windows were drawn with thick curtains.

There was another door to the conference room ten paces to the right.

The general only had one visible sidearm.

The lieutenant stood to their left, his hands folded behind his back.

It was about ten paces to the door they were brought through.

Stieg was directly behind him.

There were letters, newly opened lying on the desk.

A steel letter opener, embossed with a Swastika, lay atop the envelopes.

As Frank stopped in front of the desk, he glanced at Roy. Roy caught his look and blinked slowly.

That had been their agreed upon signal they had discussed at one point.

It meant one thing.

I'm ready.

The general said something, and Stieg began to translate, "General Rhinestadt would like to know who your commanding officer is."

Immediately, something funny came to Frank's mind, and he started to laugh.

"What is it?!" demanded Stieg.

Frank tried to stop laughing, but the thought just persisted and made their whole situation funnier.

"What is it, Battle?" asked Stieg, "What is so funny?"

Even Roy looked confused, which was fine, because then he wouldn't give their plan away.

"It's just, there's these two comedians...." Frank tried to speak between bursts of laughter, wondering himself, where this was coming from, "I don't know if you've heard of them...Abbott and Costello..."

The look on the general's face was of complete confusion.

Frank continued, "They have a skit...who's on first...you see..." Frank leaned over the desk, doubling over from laughter, "Who's on first!"

Grabbing the letter opener, Frank spun around, aiming high because Stieg was taller than him. The metal sliced into the German's cheek, scoring deep, blood spraying. As he stumbled back, his hands going to his face to protect it, Frank followed up with a Golden–Gloves–trained salvo. Gut shot and then hook to the head. Officer Stieg went down in a heap.

Roy, at the moment that Frank had spun around, had leaped upon the Lieutenant, knocking him senseless enough to seize his sidearm. As Stieg collected himself, he looked up to see two Americans with German handguns trained on him and the General. He raised his hands in surrender.

"Tell the general we want his gun."

Stieg did, and the General, who looked bewildered and yet, somehow calm, handed his gun over to them. Roy took it and stuck behind his belt.

Frank pointed his gun at Stieg, "Give me your knife as well."

Stieg sighed and handed over his knife.

"Roy, keep your eye on them." Frank took the knife and walked over to the thick curtain and began to cut long strips away from it. When he had enough, he walked over to the nameless Lieutenant and placed a gag in his mouth. He then tied up the man's hands behind his back and his feet together.

Frank walked over to the doorway to the right and found it to be a small restroom with a sink and toilet. Satisfied, he dragged the officer's limp body across the room and placed him on the toilet, using more curtain strips to further secure him to the pipes and restrain his movements. When he had returned, he found that Roy had moved the general and Stieg from the desk to two chairs in the middle of the room. The General's expression was still nonplussed.

"Now what?" asked Roy.

"Now we get out of here," said Frank.

He turned his gun upon Stieg.

"I want you to call the general's driver here. If more than one per-son shows up through that door...well...you understand don't you?"

Stieg nodded, his right hand holding a handkerchief to his bleeding cheek.

"Roy, hand him the phone."

While Roy did it, Frank began to tear down the massive map on the wall that detailed German and Allied positions. He then folded the pieces together into manageable sizes.

"What are you doing?" Roy asked.

"I'm making us heroes, Roy...making us heroes."

Chapter 6
Celebrity Head

Stieg called the driver to come into the conference room. Roy quickly knocked the man unconscious before he could react, took off the man's uniform, and put it on.

Frank's head was spinning as he ripped the telephone wires out of the wall. Thus isolating those inside from calling out an alarm.

He was sure that the two of them would be caught the moment they walked out of the conference room. However, there was no one in the hallway. Frank had his gun pointed at both the general and Stieg, with Roy in the lead, wearing the driver's uniform. Frank was dressed in the lieutenant's uniform, which wasn't hard as they were approximately the same size, while Stieg wore his uniform. With Stieg's cap on, it was hard to distinguish him from a German. Besides, the SS on the lapels, Frank figured, did much to drive eyes away from his face. As a final measure of safety, Frank had the general turn over the key to the room, with which he locked behind them after they left.

Roy had a good memory for places, and he led them without hesitation directly to the entrance of the building. As they exited, Frank saw the General's car sitting before them, idling. Fortune, or God, or maybe it was just the Padre, was smiling on them, Frank thought to himself as they walked down the steps toward the car.

None of the sentries gave them a second glance after they saluted the General. The general did his part and saluted back without incident.

So far...so good.

As Roy took his place behind the steering wheel, Frank sat in the back, which was spacious enough for all three men. He bid the general to sit in the middle, with Stieg on the outside. Then with his gun firmly planted in the general's gut, he said to Roy, "Ok, Roy, let's get moving."

While awaiting the arrival of the general's driver, Roy had located some maps of the local area as it was delineated by distance from the front line. According to the maps, they were ten miles behind the front line, ten miles that they could cross within minutes by means of the general's car.

Frank patted his uniform chest. Underneath the uniform was the massive map that they had torn down and folded into smaller more functional pieces. That map, Frank was sure, was going to be instrumental in breaking through the German lines. If he and Roy could get it to their CO, then this could be a pivotal moment for the Allies.

Frank never saw himself as a hero.

He never saw himself as much of anything above what his rank required of him.

But he felt that *something* or *someone* was guiding events even now.

Especially now.

If there was one thing that he had learned from Napoleon Hill's book, it was that opportunity comes but once. Never twice. If you don't seize upon it, then you will be doubly hard pressed to find it again.

To put it plainly, this was nothing more than opportunity dropped into his lap. He had to do this. There was no way around it.

Is it worth my life?

After a moment's reflection, he had his answer.

Yes.

Roy was good with maps. That was something that Frank had learned the first day of training with him at their post. He drove down the street, in a northern direction, until he reached the first intersection. Turning left, he began moving west.

"*Du bist fett*," said the general.

"What'd he say?" asked Frank.

Stieg looked at him with a calm look on his face, "He said that you are bold."

"Ich bewundere, dass ein Soldat," he continued, now looking Frank in the eye.

"I admire that in a soldier," translated Stieg.

"Tell him that he's a pretty cool customer himself. I'm surprised he hasn't panicked at this point," replied Frank.

Stieg translated, and the general smirked.

"Wird man nicht General des Dritten Reiches von pissing an sich selbst in diesen Situationen."

"One does not become General of the Third Reich by pissing on oneself in these situations."

Frank smiled to himself, "General...I have to hand it to you...you've got balls."

Stieg translated, and the general laughed.

"Ich bin ein general. Ich interessiere mich für meinen großen Bällen bekannt!"

"I'm a General. I'm known for my big balls!"

Frank couldn't help but chuckle at this.

"So I'm curious...General...how do you see this playing out?"

Stieg translated and the general sighed, thought for a moment, and then said, *"Ich sehe, Sie andernfalls zu Ihrem Ziel zu erreichen. Ich sehe, Sie werden wieder eingefangen. Ich sehe mich verhindert, dass Ihre sofortige Ausführung."*

"I see you failing to reach your objective. I see you being captured again. I see me preventing your immediate execution."

"And why, my good general, would you do a thing like that?"

Stieg translated and the general looked into the distance, not particularly focusing on one thing. Then he spoke, *"Als ich ein Kind war, wuchs ich mit den Ruhm des Vaterlandes in meinem Hause, in meiner Kirche, in meiner Schule. Ich kämpfte im ersten Weltkrieg. Ich habe gelernt, dass es so etwas wie ein ehrlicher Mann, ein Krieger, ein Mann, der seinen Grund geschenkt werden sollte. Er sollte, sei er Freund oder Feind, da Ehre für seine Tapferkeit und Mut werden. Er sollte Auszeichnung für seine Hingabe an seine Mission, sein Kommandeur, sein Land gegeben werden. Sie sind wie ein Mann, Frank Battle. Wie ist Ihr Begleiter. Wenn Sie wieder eingefangen werden, werde ich persönlich zu Ihrem Schutz vor denen, die Sie ausführen sehen würde."*

Stieg listened intently, and when the general finished, he addressed Frank solemnly,

"When I was a child, I grew up with the glory of the Fatherland in my home, in my church, in my school. I joined the service when I was young. I fought in the first Great War. I have learned that there is such a thing as an honorable man, a warrior man, who should be given his due. He should, be he friend or foe, be given honor for his bravery and courage. He should be given honor for his dedication to his mission, to his commander, to his country. You are such a man, Frank Battle. As is your companion. When you are recaptured, I will personally see to your protection from those who would execute you."

Frank smiled at the general's offer, "Well then...I guess we'll have to make sure we don't get recaptured. Isn't that right, Roy?"

"Yep," Roy answered, eyes intent on the road and surroundings.

They had already passed three checkpoints.

Frank was sure that the familiarity of the general's car had been the reason they had sailed through without being stopped. Then a thought occurred to him.

"Roy, pull over a second."

"Sure thing," he responded.

The car came to a stop on a deserted street.

"How far do you figure we are from the front, Roy?"

Roy was examining his map, "I'd say three miles at most. If we just keep going in this direction." He motioned with his right hand the direction that they had been traveling.

"Good," Frank fixed his eye upon the general, "Do you have any maps that locate the nearest pillbox closest to the front?"

Roy rummaged through his maps for a moment until he stopped, "Yep! Got it right here! All the pillboxes that are on the front!"

"How close are we to the one closest to the line?"

Roy did the mental calculations in his head and then answered, "About four miles away, in the same direction. In fact, I'm pretty sure I can drive us there! The layout of this city isn't hard once you've got a map to it."

The general met Frank's stare, and seemed to realize what Frank was thinking. The expression on his face changed to one of immense admiration. *"Hervorragende Denken, Lieutenant Battle! Jetzt bist du wie ein General Denken!"*

Stieg smiled when he heard this, and Frank heard admiration in his voice.

"Excellent thinking, Lieutenant Battle! Now you are thinking like a general!" Stieg added, "I think the General likes you, Battle. This will prove interesting, no?"

Frank ignored the comment, "Roy, can you get us within a mile of that pillbox?"

"Sure, Frank, what do you have in mind?"

"I'm thinking of a real coup, Roy. A real coup."

Despite his plans, Frank had one nagging sensation at the back of his skull. During OCS, one night he went out drinking with the other candidates. One of them, a guy by the name of Johnny Fellem, was considered the life of the party. Fellem was the one who was responsible for organizing these little parties. He always had a drinking game for the rest to play. One drinking game was called Celebrity Heads. Everyone wrote down a celebrity name on a card, and then shuffled the deck, passed out the cards, and placed it on their foreheads without looking at it. Then they had to figure out what celebrity they were. Every wrong answer deserved another drink.

Frank was particularly bad at that game. He remembered drinking a whole lot and not winning.

He felt like that now.

The car had been stopped at a checkpoint instead of being waved through.

Blood pounded in his ears as the German soldier motioned with his hand for Roy to lower the window so he could speak to him.

"Roy..." Frank said softly.

"Yeah?" Roy whispered back.

"Do what you have to. We have to get to that pillbox. Understand?"

"Yep," Roy acknowledged.

There were three other Germans standing on Frank's side of the car.

Suddenly, Stieg spoke, "Lieutenant Battle, you are going to have to now live up to your namesake, yes?" He looked at Frank with a knowing smile on his face.

Battle realized Stieg was right.

It was Showtime.

"Let's do this, Roy!" Frank declared, opening his rear passenger door which was opposite of Roy.

As Frank stepped out, the three German soldiers looked in his direction, burp guns slung around their shoulders. They were each smoking a cigarette, holding them in that European fashion between the index and middle finger. They had no reason to think anything out of the ordinary. They looked at him, and then noticing his lapels and the rank on them, saluted.

Everything slowed.

Time began to crawl for Frank as he tasted copper in his mouth for the second time in his life.

The first time had been when he had been avoiding the 88mm shells ripping the schoolhouse apart. That was a completely nerve–shattering experience.

That taste in his mouth?

He knew it because of what his training CO had taught him in the training field.

"That's a Fear gentleman. That's what Fear tastes like. Copper. Like you just swallowed a mouthful of pennies. Get used to it."

Copper filled his mouth.

His heart pounded so loudly, he almost didn't hear Roy's gun go off, as Roy shot the German soldier point–blank in the head. It was such a tiny sound to him. Not even a *bang*. More like a *pop*. Like a tiny balloon that was dying. Out of the corner of his eye, Frank saw the soldier's head blossom in blood and brains.

He didn't hesitate.

He aimed his pistol at the Germans who were shocked and confused.

One.

Pop.

Frank's excellent marksmanship served him well that moment. A bullet between the eyes at twenty paces.

Two.

Pop.

The second German was trying to raise his gun to fire at Frank when Frank's bullet found a place in his chest.

Frank fired again.

Pop.

A second bullet took the man's life from him.

There was a dim registration of metallic *thunk...thunk...thunk* noises.

It was then Frank realized that the third German soldier had fired upon him, and would have hit him cleanly, if it weren't for the reinforced doors of the General's car. Frank had been standing behind the car door the entire...was it just a few seconds now?

How long had he been standing there?

It felt like hours.

As he drew down on the third soldier, Frank exhaled, realizing that he had been holding his breath. Before he could squeeze the trigger, the soldier went down in a heap, brought down by gunfire from another direction.

Roy.

He looked across the car and saw Roy had gotten out of the car and opened fire on the last soldier. It was a good thing he had. Frank didn't know if he would have survived against a burp gun.

"Thanks, Roy."

"Yep," Roy acknowledged.

As they returned to their seats, Stieg said, "You impress me once again, Lieutenant Battle. You live up to your namesake. It takes a brave soul to stand up to three men at once. Even if one uses subterfuge."

Frank shrugged, "Stieg, I'm done impressing you. I really don't give a damn anymore about that. I just want to get back to my people."

"Fair enough, Battle. Fair enough."

Roy drove the general's car through the checkpoint and on toward their target destination.

The pillbox.

Chapter 7
Pillbox Redux

Roy stopped the car and turned around to face Frank.

"Frank, it's about a hundred yards ahead of us." He pointed with his left, his right holding his gun. He glanced at the general and Stieg.

Both men looked like they were disinterested in what Roy had to say. It was Frank they were both focused on. Actually, it was Frank who everyone was looking at, as though Roy had just been along for the ride. Once again, and not for the first time, Frank wondered about his training CO's comments he had made to him one evening about Frank's mettle.

They had been in class, in a lecture about the distinguishing elements of a leader versus a follower and what it took to be a leader in the US Army.

"It takes special man to be an officer, gentlemen," the CO said. "It requires, above all, a willingness to have vision, a plan, of your mission objectives...and to stick to that plan. You have to have vision and dedication. If you cannot dedicate yourself to the mission, then you will not succeed as a leader. Do I make myself clear?"

There was a chorus of "Yes, sir!"

"When you are given a mission by your CO, you must have the dedication to stick to that mission, come hell or high water. You must stick to that mission, because that is your purpose in life! Your only purpose is that mission. Your only purpose is completion of that mission. That is what you are to do! Are we clear?"

Another chorus of "Yes, sir!"

After the class, the CO had pulled Frank to the side.

"Battle," he began, "I want you to know that you are someone that is not like the other candidates in this program. I can see it in your eyes, your face, your demeanor."

"What do you mean, sir?" Frank asked.

"You have top–tier leadership written all over you. I don't expect it to be long before you are promoted from 2nd LT to higher ranks. You've got that fire that speaks to men under you. They will follow you. Even into hell...they will follow you."

Now, as they exited the car, that last sentence reverberated in his head.

Even into hell...they will follow you.

Is that where he was leading Roy? Into hell? No, that wasn't his intention. His plan was simple. Get the maps that reveal the German artillery to his CO. Once they made it to the pillbox, then Roy could raise their troops on the radio, and the two of them would sit tight until the Calvary came riding in. In addition, Frank would have a general to hand over to his superiors. The general was nothing more than insurance and icing on the cake, as far as Frank was concerned.

The general and Stieg both were compliant with his directions as they began moving toward the pillbox.

"No sudden moves. Let the general get us in there, and then I want you two to find a corner and stay put."

Stieg translated this to the general.

The General replied, "*Dies sollte interessant sein! Sehr gut, Herr Leutnant Battle, ich werde Ihr Spiel!*"

Frank looked at Stieg, who smiled and said, "He said 'This should be interesting! Very well, Lieutenant Battle, I shall play your game!'"

"It's not a game, Stieg," said Frank, "I don't play games. And if I do, I play to win."

"Point taken," replied Stieg, "Lieutenant Battle, you are a worthy opponent. I am thrilled beyond measure to have met someone like you."

Frank didn't know if that was a compliment or if he was making fun.

It didn't matter.

"Just get the general to get us inside. Understand?"

"Understood, Frank Battle."

Obediently, Stieg and the general exited the car, with Roy covering them with a burp gun he had picked up off one of the dead Germans at the checkpoint they had just left. Frank looked into the sky, measuring the time until the sun would begin its decline. He reckoned they had about three hours left till sunset. Would it be enough to marshal an offensive from the Allied side to rescue them? But before that, they had to get inside that pillbox.

He gestured with his Luger in the direction of the structure, "Let's go gentlemen, daylight's burning."

The general led their procession. He walked with a calmness and certainty that Frank wondered if they weren't actually walking into a well–laid trap by the SS. The old man was cool as ice!

How can he do that? He's acting like this is a stroll in the park, not the front line of a war.

Yet, despite being impressed by the general's unruffled demeanor, there was a part of Frank that would not let him forget that the general was the enemy. He was part of the military that had raped Poland, France, Britain, and countless other countries. His pride was in his country's ability to dominate and destroy another population's government, military, and society.

It was those thoughts that emboldened Frank as he walked behind Stieg and the general.

Fifty paces to the Pillbox.

Suddenly, there was a call from the structure, and a gun barrel appeared, aiming at them.

"*Wer ist da?*"

Stieg answered, "*Haben Sie nicht erkennen, ein SS–Offizier mit General Rhinestadt?*"

Frank wasn't sure what he said, but a moment later, the door to the pillbox opened and three Germans filed out, saluting as the general approached.

General Rhinestadt returned the salute and glanced back at Frank. There was a look in his eye that transcended any language barrier.

Let the game begin!

A slight sneer that appeared on his face, and Frank reacted immediately. "Get in there, Roy!" he shouted.

In a moment, everything was pandemonium. Roy leapt in front of the general, releasing a spray of bullets upon whoever else was in the pillbox. Seeing what the general was about to do, Frank rushed forward, grabbing him from behind, and stopping him from escaping into the pillbox and locking Frank outside with the German soldiers.

Clever fox!

Stieg tried to get to the general first, but Frank was quicker. Now they were backing up into the open doorway of the pillbox, with a Luger pressed against the general's temple. The three German soldiers were paralyzed with indecision. Which was exactly what Frank wanted. Stieg had managed to step away from them, and was screaming for the soldiers to do something. But the look on their faces said that they were terrified of making a mistake, more so than of the SS officer screaming at them.

"Stieg!" Frank called out.

"*Ja?*" The expression on his face was one of pure frustration.

"Do you want to join us in here? Protect your general? Or will you risk it out there, when my guys come pouring through the streets toward this position?"

"I believe you are an honorable man, Frank Battle. You will not kill the general. He is too valuable to your officers. So let it be a race, to see who will claim the prize!" There was a bit of a mad gleam in the man's eye.

He really thinks this is some kind of game!

Frank, without warning, aimed his Luger at the soldier nearest Stieg and fired, killing the soldier instantly. The blood from the bullets sprayed across Stieg's face.

That's so he knows that I'm serious.

Stieg looked up from the dead man that lay on the ground next to him. The look in his eye was colder now.

"It's not a game, Stieg. I play to win."

When Stieg answered, his voice had lost all of its joviality and slap–you–on–the–back–pal tone and inflection. Instead, his voice was flat and low.

"So do I, Frank Battle. So do I." He turned and fled.

Frank pulled the general with him backwards into the pillbox, and Roy slammed the door shut.

"Now what Frank?" Roy asked, as he secured the general's hands behind his back and made him sit in a chair in the corner.

"Get on the radio and find our frequency. Let them know that we have a General Rhinestadt in addition to valuable maps that detail troop positions along the Western German Front."

"Then what?"

"Then tell them to get their asses here yesterday!"

"Will do."

As Roy started fiddling with the German radio, seeking the frequency, Frank took stock of their inventory. Weapons, ammunition, rations, enough to hold out for a while at least. Satisfied, he walked over to the general and checked the man's bonds to ensure that they were secure.

A moment later, he heard the first thud against the reinforced door. Stieg was back more quickly than he had expected.

It begins.

He picked up the heavy machine gun and propped it into the gun slot. Outside, he could already see a squad of Germans who were taking up a position from where they could attack the door.

Frank swallowed, squinted, and felt himself go numb.

It's them or me. It's them or me.

With that thought, he squeezed off the first few rounds of ammunition, cutting the squad down where they stood. They obviously hadn't thought that they would become targets so quickly. Their mistake.

No...it was Stieg's mistake.

Stieg led these men to their death.

Frank stared at the still forms of five Germans, now lying in the streets, their blood issuing from their dying bodies, and wondered if Stieg cared about his men. Or were they nothing more than a means to an objective? Was that what being a commander really was? A position where you used your men as tools to accomplish the objective, and to Hell with their lives?

But this is war, he reminded himself.

As another squad of Germans moved into view, Frank exhaled again, realizing that he had been holding his breath, and squinted, aimed, and squeezed the trigger.

This is war. God help me. This is war.

Roy was beside him now, picking up another weapon and taking a position to fire at their attackers.

"I got through, Frank! Our boys are coming! They're on the way! We just got to hold out!"

Frank felt his spirits lift.

Soon he could turn over the pieces of the map that he had stuffed under his shirt. Even now, he could feel their combined pieces like so much padding down his front.

Soon...soon I can turn this map over.

Another German came into view, and Frank cut him down.

This is war.

That phrase repeated itself in Frank's head over and over. Like a mantra, it both justified his actions and soothed his conscience. He kept repeating to himself over and over, every time a German's life was taken by his gunfire, he repeated it.

This is war. This is war. This is war.

Time stretched into long silences punctuated by the sound of their guns and the shells that clinked on the concrete floor beneath them. It was hard to tell what happened to the time. Frank knew it was getting darker, and that was not good.

Where are our boys?

The Germans kept coming.

They didn't stop trying to take the pillbox, but Frank and Roy were too good at picking off their attackers.

For the nth time, Frank was grateful for his drill instructor that had been such a hard–ass about proper firing technique and quality of shooting grades. He had made sure that every man who was in OCS could outshoot any enlisted man's shooting record.

"It's a matter of pride, Dammit!" he would say, "I will not let my candidates lead men into the field who themselves cannot shoot the balls off a dragonfly at fifty yards!"

No one dared tell him that dragonflies didn't have balls.

Where are our boys?

Frank looked over at Roy, who was loading another clip into his weapon. Roy was so intent on his task that he didn't bother to look up.

"They're coming, Frank. I know it. They're coming."

"I hope so, Roy. I hope so."

There was a moment of stillness, and in the silence, Frank heard a shuffle behind him.

He looked behind him.

He saw the general. Not seated, but upright, with the butt of a rifled raised over his head. As the butt of the rifle crashed down onto Frank's temple, one thought had a chance to manifest before the darkness came.

I lost the game...dammit...

Chapter 8
The True Face of Evil

Frank awoke in darkness.

The fact that he awoke at all was a relief to him.

It meant, of course, that he wasn't dead.

There was no source of light in the room whatsoever, so he had to rely upon his sense of touch to try to determine what was happening to him. All he could tell at this point, was that he was sitting upright in a chair, feet bound to the legs, hands bound to the arms. It felt like a wooden chair. The wood was smooth against his bare skin.

Bare skin? I'm naked?

That thought was very unsettling to him, but he realized it was true. He could feel the cold air against his nakedness, and he wondered what the purpose was.

Is this the general's doing?

Frank strained against his bonds, but they held him tight.

"Herr Battle, the bonds are wet leather. I find those most constricting in this situation." The German voice was very close, behind him perhaps. It was such a casual tone, as if the man were playing a game of poker with him.

Frank knew the owner of the voice without needing to ask.

Stieg.

Frank said nothing, not wanting to give him the pleasure of conversation.

"Are you a little confused, yes? Dismayed? The General did keep his promise. You will not be executed, and I will make sure that happens."

Now Frank couldn't contain himself, and as he opened his mouth, his voice was parched and raspy, "Why?"

"I will answer that at the conclusion of our session today, Herr Battle."

Great, now he's going to play games with my head.

"Oh, I can't wait for this to be over then," Frank fired off sarcastically.

There was a moment of silence, and in that silence, Frank could *hear* the man smile. "Herr Battle, you have never spoken truer words."

There was a click of a wall switch behind him, and suddenly, Frank was bathed in solitary column of light. It made his eyes water as they tried to adjust to the sudden change. He found himself trying to wipe his eyes clear of the tears, but he couldn't of course, due to the leather bonds around his wrists. As his eyes adjusted to the light, he saw that he was indeed naked, strapped to a high—backed wooden chair with arms. There was also a tight leather band across his chest that he hadn't realized before.

But that wasn't what chilled him.

It was the fact that his feet were in a small tub filled with about three inches of water.

What the hell?

As he looked, he then noticed one other thing. There were some kind of wires, or electrodes taped to the inside of each thigh.

The leather band around his chest was nowhere as constricting as the feeling that threatened to overwhelm him at that moment.

"What the hell do you think you're doing?" Frank demanded.

"Doing?" replied Stieg, "I haven't done anything. We're just having a conversation, Herr Battle."

"Let me out of here! I demand it!"

There was a deep throaty laughter, "You made demands? You arrogant American Cowboys! Always sticking your noses in where it doesn't belong! Do you think that you are in any position to make demands here? Demands of me?"

"You can't do this to me! The Geneva Convention..."

"Does not exist in *my* world, Herr Battle."

Frank stopped. *His world? What the hell does that mean?*

As if reading his thoughts, Stieg continued, and as he spoke, his voice moved from behind Frank to the right side, just outside the edge of the column of light.

"Herr Battle, you are in a special place. You are alive, but you are also dead. You are registered as a Prisoner, but you fall under MY jurisdiction directly. It is a gift, you see, from General Rhinestadt. Now understand, Herr Battle, that he is appreciative of your willingness to spare his life, so in return, he has spared yours. Yet he is not a man without a sense of justice and retribution. After what you did to me... well, let us just say that, you are a gift to me."

"I prefer someone else."

"Battle, there is no one else..." Stieg laughed, "You see...I am known by my reputation in the SS. They call me the Wolf. You are mine now."

Frank could see Stieg, the Wolf, only by the fiery orange glow of the cigarette he held in his hand as he walked around him, remaining in the shadows, a disembodied voice. Taunting and in complete control, Frank realized.

The floating cigarette stopped about five feet away, directly in front of him.

"There's just me, Herr Battle."

Frank said nothing.

"Nothing smart–ass to say? Hmm?"

Frank was silent, looking at his lap, wondering how much this was going to hurt.

"Good...then perhaps you will be honest with me."

"I won't tell you anything about the military."

The cigarette floated as he waved away that particular comment as irrelevant, "I could care less about your troop movement, Herr Battle."

Then what does he want from me?

"We will gain the upper hand over the invaders soon enough. I really could, as you Americans say 'give a rat's ass' about that."

Frank was silent.

Don't give him the satisfaction.

"Nothing to say? Hmm?"

Frank remained silent.

"Very well...I think it is time for us to begin. You see those wires attached to your person?"

Frank got very cold inside. Fear threatened to overwhelm him, but somehow, he kept it in check.

"Our behavioral scientists have learned many things from a man named Pavlov. I don't suppose you've heard of him, no?"

Frank said nothing.

"No? Well, it doesn't matter. Pavlov discovered some amazing things about the body and behavior through a process called conditioning."

Frank suddenly couldn't contain himself, "If you're going to fry me...go ahead and do it! You damn dirty Kraut!"

There was a click on the wall in front of him, and suddenly pain unlike anything he had ever known filled his world.

Everything ceased to be.

There was only a numbing blinding arc of agony that coursed through his body. His jaws clenched. His eyelids fluttered. His heart thundered in his ears.

Then it was over.

Frank gasped.

"That was three seconds, Herr Battle. I suggest you do not interrupt me again, yes?"

Frank didn't answer.

I can't go through that again. I just can't.

"How?" he rasped as he caught his breath, "How can you do this? The Geneva Convention forbids..."

"I told you, Herr Battle," he paused as the cigarette fell to the ground, was crushed under his foot, and another one was lit, "You belong to me now. As far as the general knows, you are being interrogated by the Geneva Convention rules."

"But you're cheating!" Frank blurted.

"Frank...Frank...Frank..." The Wolf said, "Now we come, in a round–about way, to today's topic, which is this...there are no rules anymore. The old ones do not apply."

"What do you mean?"

"Have you ever heard of a man named Friedrich Nietzsche?"

"No..."

"Ahh...the quality of American education...you are truly becoming a dumb nation. No wonder it falls to us in Europe to enlighten you as to the coming age."

"What are you talking about?"

"I attended one of your American universities, you know...Studied psychology. I have a rather extensive knowledge of how the mind works and how it develops. That is, of course, where I learned of Pavlov and the process of conditioning."

"Why are you telling me this?" Frank's tone was getting short.

Suddenly, pain bloomed in his legs again.

His world shrank to a single moment of existence.

Then it was over.

"That was two seconds...now...with each session...I will *teach* you how to respond appropriately...do you understand?"

Frank said nothing as drool fell from his mouth.

His head was a storm of clouds preventing any clear thought to shine through.

"Yes...of course you do."

Frank struggled to bring a coherent thought together, but nothing in his head worked.

After a long moment of silence, the Wolf stepped forward into the light, looking down at him. Frank struggled to raise his head. All he saw was the Wolf's face in shadow.

A word escaped from Frank's lips...barely audible.

The Wolf leaned down, and Frank saw him clearly now, an uncovered thick angry row of black stitches decorated the left cheek of the man's face. But it was still the eyes that drew Frank in. Cold. Black. Penetrating. Raging.

And completely insane.

"Say that again?" said the Wolf.

This time, the word that passed through Frank's lips actually reached his own ears.

"Why?"

The Wolf grinned, and Frank thought distantly, of the story of Little Red Riding Hood.

"I will leave you with two ideas to contemplate until our next session, Herr Battle. Idea Number One: There are no rules except what you make. Idea Number Two: Might makes right."

Frank's voice was starting to return.

"I don't understand..." he rasped.

"You will...Herr Battle...you will."

A hood had been placed over Frank's head, and he was taken from his room of torture to another cell, where there was a metal cot bolted to the floor, a thin blanket and a metal toilet. Frank was so weak; they had to place him on the cot. He curled up into a ball with the blanket wrapped around him.

Sleep came quickly as exhaustion filled his every muscle.

When he opened his eyes, he didn't know what time it was, because there was no window to his cell. It could have been midnight or noon for all he knew.

Time had disappeared.

There was a plastic bottle of water that had been set at the foot of the cot. As Frank drank it slowly, he tried to clear his head and organize his thoughts.

It was hard.

The Wolf's face kept dominating his thoughts. Frank had come over here with the image of Hitler being the malevolent force behind the Nazi conquest.

That no longer held true for him.

Frank now knew the true face of Evil.

No rules and might makes right. What did he mean by that? I've never heard that before. It's insane.

Before he could think on it any further, the door to his cell opened, a German soldier came in and tossed him a black hood.

Frank put it on, realizing that they still hadn't given him his clothes back.

How long? Oh God...how long is this going to take?

"God is dead," declared the Wolf.

Frank was back in the chair, strapped in and wired for pain.

"What do you mean?" asked Frank.

"This is Nietzsche's foundational statement. To truly grasp the ideas that follow...Herr Battle, you must accept that God is dead."

"That's preposterous."

"Is it?" The Wolf leaned down and smirked, "If your God is alive, he's pretty impotent in the face of the Third Reich. He has done nothing to stop us. There are no angels coming to slay the German army. We have unfettered power. We are a force of lightening on the earth. Soon...all will be swept away by our might and we will rebuild this world in a glorious way."

Frank couldn't conceal a short laugh, "You're Looney!"

"No...Herr Battle, I am not delusional...you are the one clinging to old belief systems that do not work and have not worked for centuries! Do you believe in God, Herr Battle?"

It was a question that Frank knew was going to come up. He had considered his conversation with the Padre. He had thought about being raised in the small church in his hometown of Dayton Ohio. He didn't have a persistent belief in God per se...it was more of a...feeling...that there was someone watching over him. That feeling had been growing as of late.

His hesitation was all that the Wolf needed, "I see it in your eyes, Herr Battle. You struggle with the concept of God. As did Nietzsche, until he had an epiphany one day, that God was truly dead."

"How is that possible?" Frank asked.

"Because we killed Him," the Wolf answered.

"We did?" replied Frank.

"You have already done so in your unbelief, this very moment, Herr Battle! Do you not see?"

"But..."

"Understand this...philosophically...logically...God is an untenable idea. He doesn't make sense rationally. If He did, then wouldn't the world be a better place?"

Frank had heard that particular argument, after a fashion, before. He didn't know what to say in response.

"But instead, we are in a world filled with Jews and Blacks and Gypsies and Queers. We are in a world that is corrupted from within by the genetic trash. We Germans are merely building a world where only the beautiful will be accepted. What is wrong with that, Herr Battle? What is wrong with living in a beautiful world?"

Frank said nothing.

"If you accept that God is dead...because Man killed him...because He was just an invention of Man to begin with...then you can accept the True Power of Man."

"The True Power?" Frank echoed.

"Yes!" The Wolf's dark eyes gleamed with fervor, "The Will to Power! The absolute Truth that Man has the Power to forge his own destiny! He has the Power to make his own rules! He has the Power to enforce his Will on the world to create what He chooses to create! That is the Will to Power! The ability to self–create your own World! Since God is dead...there are no rules binding Man except what Man has the Will to Power to create! Thus...Might makes Right!"

It made sense...if one accepted that God was dead.

Something was bothering him though...he couldn't place his finger on it...

The Wolf continued, "Do you see the points I'm trying to make, Herr Battle? They are logical, yes?"

Logical...yes...but there was something...

Then Frank realized what it was...it hit him like freight train, shaking him to the core...it was a single thought...and he didn't know if it came from him...or somewhere else...

Just because a thing is logical...doesn't make it moral...

With that thought, he realized what the Wolf was doing to him. He was trying to turn him. What a better prize for an SS officer, than to turn an enemy to his way of thought and ideas. This wasn't a torture session just for torture's sake. It was a place of conversion. He was trying to promote the ideas that were apparently at the heart of the Nazi regime.

In a way, Frank thought, *the Wolf is trying to justify his own existence.*

This thought emboldened him.

The question is...will I break?

There was something in Frank's face that spoke of his internal revelation. The Wolf saw it and said, "What is it? You've just realized something, Herr Battle. Do you see the Truth of what I'm saying? Do you understand the righteousness of our cause?"

Frank collected his thoughts for a moment before he said, "What I understand, Wolf, is that *you* are trying to *turn* me. *You* are trying to justify your existence. *You* are trying to defend the actions of nation that are built upon ideas of what I consider to be a deranged man! *You*, sir, are not righteous! *You are evil!*"

The Wolf stepped back, his face dark with fury. He turned away from the column of light and toward the wall where Frank knew a switch lay.

Frank braced himself.

He had one last thought before the electricity flooded his body and filled his mind with agony.

Dear God...if you're there...help me...

It was a full day, Frank reckoned, before he regained a sense of con-sciousness. When he finally awoke clear—headed on his metal cot, he found his clothes were lying folded on the floor beside him.

He dressed slowly.

The water bottle that he had drained had been refilled.

There was a bowl of cold porridge resting on a tray at the foot of the door.

Frank devoured the food and was left wanting more.

I suppose I better get used to the hunger.

He sat on the cot, wrapped the thin blanket around him, trying to keep warm in the cold, and thought about his conversation with the Wolf.

There was so much there to think about. Something occurred to him as he chewed over the German's words. He had just been given the reason why they were doing what they were doing. They believed they were right. They believed that they were morally right. To them... they weren't evil. They were righteous. To them...they were...acting in a righteous manner.

But if God were dead...wouldn't that mean that no one is right? No one is wrong?

If God were dead...then...morality disappears.

The door to cell opened and the Wolf stood there.

Frank tensed.

"You are being moved...Congratulations...Per General Rhinestadt, you will be joining your fellow escapee on the way to a holding camp."

Roy was alive? Up to this moment, Frank had hardly thought of Roy, except to assume he was dead.

"Someone will bring you shoes."

The door began to close, and then it re–opened.

Frank froze.

The Wolf stared at him with baleful eyes, "Herr Battle, we shall continue our discussions. I am not done with you..."

The door closed...and Frank shivered.

But not from the cold in the room.

The man known as the Wolf smiled to himself as he left the American to wonder about his fate. The guards kept their eyes forward, not daring to let them wander upon The Wolf's face as he passed them in the hallway. No, they didn't want his attention. They had heard the stories. Stories that he had actually planted in the first place.

I'm sure, he thought to himself, *they all are thinking of at least two or three of my exploits when they realize who I am.* It was actually hard for him to suppress the smile on his face at the thought of the fear he invoked in these lesser men.

That was what they were.

Lesser men.

Of course, they were of the same race, the same glorious race that his Teacher, Herr Villers had taught about.

Thoughts about his Teacher took him back to a happier, even more exciting time in his life. Not that Now wasn't exciting and challenging. Of course, it was. But then...

As he entered his private office, his aide handed him a stack of reports and a cup of hot tea. The Wolf barely noticed both. He was already fifteen years in the past...

Alexander Stieg stood in the cafeteria, holding his tray as he received his meal.

The worker who placed the food on his tray, looked up cautiously, timidly, daring to meet his gaze. She was a dark–haired little Jew. Alexander forced a smile to his lips, showing a few teeth. The little Jew blanched, out of fright or embarrassment, it didn't matter. She quickly dropped her gaze back to the steeping plates of food in front of her, try-ing to forget the look she had just seen in Alexander's eyes.

She sees the Wolf, he thought with satisfaction.

Alexander turned from the food line and walked to a solitary spot at a table in the corner of the cafeteria. He ignored the stares he felt burning into his back from the upperclassmen. It was only his third week since being enrolled in this school, and Alexander would never forget the sacrifice his father made that enabled him to be there. He swore that he would make good on such a sacrifice. He would make his father proud.

"Hey! Stieg!" a rough voice shook him out of his reverie.

Alexander looked up at the speaker, Konrad, he thought the boy's name was. The upperclassman was standing over him, flanked by three of his companions. The look of malice was unmistakable in Konrad's eyes. Alexander had encountered this before. Not in this place, no...far from here. In a place these city–boys had no idea existed. Alexander tried to conceal his disdain for Konrad, but he knew he failed when the upperclassman's eyes widened in anger.

"Are you being disrespectful?" taunted Konrad. "You should know by now...that we upperclassmen deserve respect! Respect you fail to give!"

Yes...Alexander had seen this before...in the face of a snarling wolf, half–starved from a winter hunger, mindless bluster. His father had taught him then how to deal with such a beast. You did it through strength.

Konrad leaned over, placing his hands flat against the table, a swatch of blonde hair hanging down over his clear blue eyes. His com-panions in this very public display of bullying snickered to each other. Like the simpering pack of hind–sniffers they were, thought Alexander.

The fool didn't even notice that Alexander's hand wrapped around his fork while he held his gaze. The next moment, Alexander drove the

fork into the upperclassman's right hand, hearing the sound of snap-
ping bone and feeling the sudden warm splash of blood spray across
his face.

Konrad's eyes doubled in size as he began his screams, pulling his
bloodied hand close to him with his other good hand. Before he could
even stumble back, Alexander drove the fork into Konrad's other hand,
feeling the metal tines dig deep into the flesh. The simpering hind–
sniffers backed away in confusion and disbelief.

Alexander kicked Konrad's right knee, hearing it dislocate as it
snapped, and the boy went down. Alexander lunged upon him, strad-
dling the boy's upper body, as he sat on his chest. Alexander looked
into the upperclassman's face, a mask of fear and uncertainty.

Alexander liked that look.

In fact, he craved it.

"So you're my better?" Alexander mocked. Konrad's eyes were
wide with fright, and he shook his head ever so slightly, denying what
had come out of his own mouth just moments before.

"No?" said Alexander, "Then, if I'm not your subordinate, and I have
the position of power here...that must mean that I'm your Master!"
With that, Alexander brought his right fist down, hitting the boy's face
with a meaty *thwak*! Alexander didn't look around, but he heard the
sudden gasps from those who were gathered around.

*I wonder if they've ever seen a true display of Herr Nietzsche's phi-
losophies and principles in action. Today, they will.*

Another punch brought a groan from Konrad, and Alexander
leaned over, "Say it! Say I'm your master! Say it!"

The upperclassman still had some reserve of pride. He shook his
head.

Alexander rained more punches upon the boy, each one punctuated by "Say it! Say it!"

Each punch brought a fresh spurt of blood from the boy's mouth
and his face was a mass of welters and cuts and freshly–forming bruises.

Time disappeared for Alexander.

The crowd disappeared.

Everything disappeared, except Konrad and the pitiful fool's resistance to recognizing that he was beaten. Finally, after what seemed like
thirty–or–so blows, Konrad's swollen face and lips mumbled something.

Alexander smiled, "No one can hear you, Konrad. Speak up!"

This time, Konrad did speak, though his speech was thick and slow from the pain, "You are my master."

Satisfied, Alexander rose off the boy and looked into the faces of the students that had surrounded them. There were boys and girls who shared this cafeteria, and every one of them had a look of shock and a particular kind of fear on their faces. It was the kind of uneasy fear that made your stomach turn into knots at realizing that you are in the presence of someone truly dangerous and menacing.

That was what pleased Alexander the most.

His mask was gone. He didn't have to pretend anymore.

They all saw, with their own eyes, what he really was.

A Wolf.

A Wolf in its prime, without mercy, without shame, full of savagery and power.

He was the Wolf that lurked in the corners of their nightmares. The lone howl that woke them from their precious deep slumbers in the middle of the night. He was their fear come true.

And he loved it.

It was later that afternoon, when the headmaster came to the door of the classroom. Alexander smiled to himself.

The looks he was already receiving from the other students spoke of how quickly his display of power and dominance was spreading throughout the hallways. Other students merely stared at him now, instead of ignoring him because he was, in their eyes, a backwater woodsman. Now they regarded him with caution and measured respect.

It was the respect that Alexander had sought after, and now he had found it.

The headmaster's eyes focused on him, and the older gentleman's face was stern and unyielding.

Alexander looked forward to this.

The teacher turned toward him and beckoned him to the door. As Alexander rose, he felt the eyes of the entire class rest upon him.

He liked that.

Notoriety, he realized, was something he could get used to rather quickly. It could add to one's power.

The teacher addressed Alexander sharply as he reached the doorway, the headmaster's gaze unmoving and firm as steel. "You will go with Headmaster Villers!"

Alexander nodded in understanding and fell in step behind the headmaster.

After a short walk down the hallway, they turned into the headmaster's office, where a pretty blonde receptionist sat amidst a mountain of papers.

The headmaster motioned for him to follow into his inner chambers, where Villers stepped behind his desk and picked up a file that lay on top of it.

Alexander stood in front of the desk, as he was not given leave to actually sit yet. His father's lessons in obedience were going to pay off, he realized. Everything that his father had taught him, about people, animals, and the world, were turning out to be true.

Villers sat down, adjusted his spectacles on his nose, and studied the file before him.

Alexander stood silently, eyes focused, making no movement of complaint or disrespect.

Finally, Villers looked up and motioned for him to sit down.

When he did, Villers spoke, his voice deep and sharp.

"I understand that you had an *incident* in the cafeteria today with an upperclassman, a young man by the name of Konrad. It seems you have completely humiliated and severely wounded him. Both his hands are broken and his jaw is dislocated."

Alexander tried very hard to suppress a smile, but he felt it creep onto his face despite his efforts.

"So you now have a reputation here, Mr. Stieg. A rather notorious one at that."

Alexander decided to forego hiding his pleasure. Perhaps this conversation would turn out to be to his advantage.

Villers leaned forward, his stern voice somehow growing even harder, "You are a young man of violence. I see that clearly. Don't think you can fool me, Stieg."

Alexander, emboldened, said, "I just got tired of pretending to soak up all the disrespect and disdain that was aimed at me. Is that so wrong? Didn't Nietzsche say..."?

"Don't you even *think* of lecturing me!" Villers voice boomed. "You think you know what you are doing...but mark my words...you are a thug! A vandal! A scoundrel!"

Alexander felt his smile melt away like a snowball in the blazing summer sun. Anger bloomed in his chest.

Villers continued, "The truth is...boys like you are as plentiful as cheap pennies! If you really want to live a life of a thug and scoundrel... you will do it outside of these grounds after you've been expelled!"

Now Alexander felt alarm.

His father had sacrificed so much for him to gain entrance into this boarding school and get the education he needed. Now...it seemed that it was all about to slip through his fingers. Alexander would have to return to his father's farm, empty–handed and...no...he couldn't do that.

"I have your attention now?" Villers tone lessened.

Alexander nodded.

"Good! You have a hard streak inside you. But that needs some shaping if you are going to use that hardness to your advantage."

Alexander stared. The expression on his face portrayed his confusion.

"I am a part of a growing organization, a Party, Stieg. I am con-stantly on the lookout for potential leaders of the future. I can see that you would be a strong leader...given the right kind of...guidance."

"Sir?" asked Alexander.

"You wish to have power and dominance? That is fine! But you wield it like a brutish child with no finesse or grace or purpose beyond wielding it! You obviously have little to no concept of the subtle arts of manipulation and coercion. But that will change."

"I don't understand, sir."

"You, Alexander Stieg, will become my pupil. I will teach you what you need to know to become the man you desire to be."

Alexander felt a mix of confusion and elation.

"But..." Villers held up a finger, "I have three conditions you must meet unconditionally!"

Alexander waited silently.

"First! You must do as I say...without question!"

"Yes, Headmaster."

"Second! You must have no more outbursts like the one today!"

"Yes, Headmaster."

"Third! I realize that your social skills are rather lacking. You must learn to develop allies and partners, but never friends!"

"Yes, Headmaster."

"You will report to my office every weekday at the close of school so we may begin your lessons! I will not tolerate tardiness or sloth! Do I make myself clear?"

"Yes, Headmaster."

"So you are willing to accept these conditions?"

"Without reservation, Headmaster."

"Good! Your first assignment is this: go apologize to Konrad, and make him think that you are going to be his friend."

"I don't understand, sir."

"You will, give me your undivided attention, and you will."

After that, the years in the boarding school passed quickly for Alexander Stieg. But that was only because he was so busy learning how to become something crucial to the New Order that was coming. So he learned every lesson that Villers taught him and learned them very well.

When the SS was formed, Alexander was one of its first officers.

When it was discovered that Villers, his mentor, was stealing from the Party, it was the Wolf, that paid him a visit, and left a lasting impression on him that their roles had changed. The student had now become the master.

The Wolf sat in his office, staring out the window, reminiscing about the old days. He didn't notice that the tea had grown cold in his hand.

This Battle is a challenge, he thought to himself. *Here is a man that would be quite a prize if I can break him and bring him to our side. Yes... quite a prize indeed.*

Chapter 9
Six Feet Under

After the Wolf left, the guards who remained handed Frank a canvas hood and gestured that he should put it on. Frank complied without a shred of resistance.

Hooded, he was led by the tug on the bonds that encircled his wrists. If he looked down, he could just see his feet. That was all.

Are they really taking me to Roy? Or am I headed for a firing lineup? They hood firing lineup targets don't they?

These thoughts and more whirled through Frank's brain. It was the not seeing that was most disturbing to him. It made the fear that was growing in his belly all the more palpable. He could tell when they exited the building because of the outdoor smell and the sharp drop in temperature. He could taste copper in his mouth – the taste of fear.

A rough shove on his left shoulder and vicious yank in the same direction made him stumble. With his hands tied, he couldn't catch himself. He fell face–long into crushed gravel. Crying out in pain, he shook his head, and the hood came off.

He was in a small courtyard behind the building in which he had been interrogated and held. To his right he saw a line of five Gerries standing at attention, rifles at the ready. To the right of them stood the Wolf. His bandage was removed, and the scar that Frank gave him bestowed on him an almost malevolent unintentional smile. The man could look at you and smile without smiling.

Frank looked to his left and saw a brick wall. A brick wall that was pitted with bullet holes and smeared with blood.

So this was the end.

Oh God! Help me! Help me God!

"No!" Frank cried out, *"You can't do this! The Geneva Convention..."*

The Wolf was there in a heartbeat, whispering in his ear, "There is no Geneva in my world, Frank Battle."

"No! Don't do this! It's not right!" Frank's heart was thundering in his chest, the blood pounding his ears. He couldn't breathe.

The two German soldiers that had guided him to this place of death pulled Frank to his feet and shoved him against the wall. The Wolf picked up the hood and started to place it over Frank's ashen face. He leaned close, centimeters from Frank's face and whispered so only Frank could hear, "Where is your God now?"

The Wolf pulled away and drew the hood down sharply over Frank's face.

Frank couldn't breathe.

He couldn't think beyond one singular thought.

Where is God in all of this?

He heard the Wolf call the firing line to attention, in English, no doubt to drive home his point even more.

"Aim!"

Frank was numb all over.

"Fire!"

A multitude of shots rang out, and Frank tensed, expecting the pain to come quickly and without delay.

But no pain came.

Frank fell to his knees, his bound hands catching on the rough gravel. The hood was yanked off his head, and Frank looked up into the Wolf's smiling face.

"Why?" was the only word that escaped his lips. It was the only word that dominated his mind.

The Wolf, with his scar deepening his already vicious grin, shrugged his shoulders, as if to say, "I did this on a whim." But what he said was, "Because I can, Frank Battle. I am God now. I control your life, Battle. You will come to fear me. You will come to respect me. And...if I do this correctly, you will come to worship me, Battle. I am your God."

Worship him? He must be insane!

What came out of Frank's mouth surprised even him, "My God doesn't wear a Nazi uniform!"

The Wolf smiled, "We shall see, Battle. We shall see." He turned to the nearest guard and said something in German, which Frank supposed meant, "Take him to the others."

It wasn't long before four Germans escorted him to a waiting transport vehicle. As Frank climbed into the back, he saw Roy there with other POWs. Frank took a seat next to Roy without comment. When he did open his mouth to say something, a guard ordered him in a thickly accented English, "Silence!"

So they rode in silence, and as the miles trailed behind them, Frank found himself sinking into a quagmire of emotions.

Doubt.

Despair.

Shame.

Uncertainty.

But the emotion that ruled them all was Fear. Fear of what lay ahead of them. Given The Wolf's willingness to break the rules of war, there was literally no telling what would happen to them. To him especially. That one stroke of the letter opener had gained him a mortal enemy that much was a certainty. That fact led him to consider that he might actually die at The Wolf's hands. Up to this point, Frank had maintained a healthy dose of optimism, fueled by Napoleon Hill's writings on the topic of remaining optimistic.

But now, Hill's writings were far away.

They were in another world.

They didn't fit in this world.

This world of Prisoners and Guards.

The world of Kriegies.

This world dominated by men and women who believed that the evil they were doing was right, and just, and holy. This world of...what did The Wolf say? Might makes Right. Yes, that was it. This was a world dominated by Might makes Right. A world where weakness was not only not tolerated, it was a death sentence.

As they rode in forced silence, Frank resolved to do one thing over the days to come. If there was one thing he could do...if there was one thing he had power over...and Hill's writings taught this...so maybe there was a place for it here in this world after all...Frank had power over his attitude.

He resolved to never give up.

He resolved to never surrender his will to live.

He resolved to fight The Wolf with his last breath.

He would spit in The Wolf's eye with every ounce of resistance he could muster. Even on the firing line. Even in the face of humiliation. Even in the face of certain death. He would not bow to this self–appointed "God."

He would not fear him.

He would not respect him.

He certainly would not worship him.

The Wolf was no "God" to be worshipped. He might hold Frank's life in his hands, with the ability to snuff him out like a guttering candle in a windstorm. But something came to him, from dim memory past, about fear. "Fear not the man who takes your life, but fear the one who can destroy your soul." Something like that. The Wolf could not touch his soul. He was not "God."

If there was a God, then, Frank realized, that was the being to whom he owed any kind of fear and respect.

Worship?

Well, Frank wasn't about to go that far. He had never really worshipped anything or anyone in his life. He didn't think he'd start now.

Frank was so lost in his thoughts that he didn't notice that the vehicle had stopped, and it was only when the guard barked out in rough English, "Get out! Hands up!" that he realized their journey was over. He exited the transport truck with Roy and the others. Six German soldiers with burp guns covered them. The Wolf was nowhere in sight.

A Command Officer addressed them in English, with a touch of a British accent. He pointed toward what looked like a metal cellar door. "You will wait there!"

Two German soldiers unlocked the chain on the cellar door and with loud creaking hinges, opened it. It was into that blackness that Frank and Roy and the other POWs descended. As they stepped into the darkness, Frank estimated that they were going deep underground. When they reached the bottom of the steps they were greeted by a dim light. The cellar steps led down to a cement hallway that was lit only by a single bulb every six or so feet. Frank estimated that they were at least sixty feet underground, if not more. The German who issued commands to them in broken English commanded them to stop.

Frank, for the first time, counted that, including him and Roy, there were eight POWs in all. He wondered what lay beyond the single metal door that stood at the end of this cement corridor.

"Against the wall! Hands up!" Again...more broken English.

Frank and Roy obeyed, as did the six others. They stood with their faces against the cold cement, bound hands on their heads, wondering what was coming.

More Germans appeared in the corridor and one of them carried what sounded like a jangle of keys. Frank turned his head slightly to the right and saw the guard unlock the large metal door and open it against the protestations of un–oiled hinges. The broken English voice thundered in the hallway.

"Get in!"

Beyond the doorway was a blackness that was untouched by the weak bulbs that glowed overhead. As Frank and Roy moved from light into darkness, Frank's eyes adjusted to the actual dim light that came from the ceiling of the room they were walking into. It appeared that they were in a basement type of bunker of sorts, with a high ceiling and openings at the top of the room to let in air and light. Night was fast approaching, and the dim light was dying by the moment.

There were no chairs or benches to sit upon, so Frank and Roy sat on the cement floor with their backs to the wall, and watched as the German guard who issued the broken English commands told them to be silent and make no trouble. These commands were punctuated by the slam of the metal door and the gloom that enveloped them all.

No one spoke.

The blackness seemed to swallow their willingness or ability to speak.

As they sat there, Frank fought a battle inside his mind and soul against the twin specters of Despair and Hopelessness. As the light from the outside finally vanished, the gloom inside his soul grew and grew.

The darkness swallowed up everything.

Finally, somehow, Frank passed from consciousness to dreaming.

He was in the schoolhouse, with 88mm shells ripping through the floors above. It was only a matter of time before the Krauts came upon his position with impunity. As the building around him shuddered and groaned from the shelling, Frank kept his eyes on the only way out of the room. He knew that if he ran through that door there would be Germans outside, waiting to cut him down with their burp guns. The choice was clear...stay and let the building collapse on top of him, or cut and run for cover somewhere else. The latest shell left him with dust in his eyes and mouth. Fear of being trapped by tons of masonry and wooden beams finally overpowered his sense of preservation. Frank stood up and ran for the open door...

...He was in the general's car. Germans had surrounded them, discovering their ruse. The general had a look in his eye that spoke of a cat that has finally trapped its mouse. He turned to him and spoke in perfectly clear English.

"Lieutenant, I suggest you surrender. If you fight, you will die."

Frank, not taken aback by the General's perfect English, replied as he pulled back the bolt on his sidearm, "If I die, then at least it will be at my choosing, not yours, Herr General." He opened the door to the car and raised his sidearm toward the knot of Germans aiming their guns at him. He began to fire...

...He was standing in the courtyard with crushed gravel under his feet. Before him stood a row of German's with their rifles aimed at him. The Wolf stood to the side, with his wicked smile–no–smile beaming.

"Ready!"

Where's my hood? Frank thought.

"Aim!"

Shouldn't I have a hood?

"Fire!"

Frank winced as bullets whistled around him, but none found home in his flesh. He fell to his knees, trembling.

The Wolf casually walked up to him, took him by the arm, and stood him back up.

"And again!" he called out to the firing line.

Frank was confused...What was going on?

"Ready!"

Why weren't they shooting him?

"Aim!"
Where was his hood? Shouldn't he get a hood?
"Fire!"

Frank awoke with a gasp, the sound of gunshots still ringing in his ears. It was morning; it appeared, from the light coming in from above. Frank's back and neck were sore from being hunched over all night. He had apparently fallen asleep in that position. He stood up slowly, feeling pins and needles in his legs as they struggled to awaken.

In the brighter light, he could see that they were in a rectangular room, cemented and bare, with a single electrical wire that led to an empty socket for a light bulb. Frank shivered as he realized that the winter air was reaching them down here.

He looked at Roy, and then the others.

They all had a look on their faces that spoke loudly of the twin specters that had conquered their spirits.

Despair and Hopelessness.

Chapter 10
Sardines in a Can

"Where the Hell are we?" the Preacher asked.

He wasn't a real preacher, of that, Frank was certain. But he had secretly tagged the man who could say "Jesus H Christ," and "Hell, dammit, and Goddamn," all in the same sentence without blinking an eye. He was a walking contradiction, in Frank's eyes. It didn't make sense, to be so devoted to your God, and yet have such contrary things come out of your mouth right on the heels of mentioning his name.

He had arrived with some more captured officers just a couple of days before. In that group, Frank found an old familiar face, the Judge. He sat next to him now, all of them waiting for whatever was going to happen next to happen.

The Judge explained that apparently, the Krauts had discovered the American officers and laid a merciless trap for them. When they moved into the area, the Germans unleashed crisscrossing rows of machine gun fire, only two feet high. It was brutal. When the firing stopped, it was the Judge who was the first to stand up and surrender. They had no other option.

Frank was pretty sure that his CO was catching hell about now for losing three of his top officers under him. He sure as anything wished he could be anywhere but in this dungeon. The darkness weighed on him ceaselessly. It was something that pressed down through the flesh, into his bones. This gripping darkness threatened to crush his heart, make it stop beating. But...there was an antidote.

The Preacher.

From the moment the Preacher arrived, something seemed to change in the darkness. Something lifted the darkness, somehow.

"How the hell you guys doing'?" said the Preacher, "Name's Gunner, boys. You can call me Gonorrhea if you want Jesus to burn your ass on a stick. You can call me Gunny if you want my CO to bust your ass. Or you can call me Gun. But for Jesus H Christ's sake, don't call me anything like Preacher. I hate that, may Jesus bless my mama. I ain't no damn Preacher, boys, you got me?"

And there it was. Preacher. Whether he knew it or not.

Despite the fact that he hated that name, Preacher was the name that stuck to him, tighter than white on rice.

Preacher would start up conversations in that dungeon, and somehow, Frank wasn't sure how, the time would pass quicker. Preacher would saddle up next to someone he didn't know, someone who wasn't in his company, and start a conversation that would go something like this:

"So...GI Joe...do you know our Blessed Lord Jesus as your personal Savior from the Devil stickin' a fire poker up your ass for all eternity?"

Frank, after hearing this for the umpteenth time, was ready when Preacher sat next to him.

"Well, Preacher...I know you don't like that title, but you've got it stuck to you tighter than a tick on a bull's nuts, I'd say that I don't know Jesus personally, we haven't shaken hands and all, but I'm just wonderin' if you can explain to me how He can be Lord and Savior and all that, and have all this hell happen around us?"

Preacher didn't even blink.

"I like you, sir! You are one tough nut! I can see that! You don't pull your punches, even when they hit below the belt! I'm gonna do something for you, sir! I'm gonna cogitate on your question and give you an answer, right proper, may Jesus bless my momma!"

And with that, Preacher left Frank alone.

Despite the contradictory nature of Preacher's mouth and his message, he did seem to lighten the gloom. After he had personally witnessed to every man in that dungeon, he didn't fall silent. He began to talk about the Nazis and the end of the world, the return of Jesus on a white horse. He believed that Hitler was the Anti–Christ and Patton was Jesus' personal point man in this conflict of what he called, "heavenly powers and thrones." Frank didn't know what to make of all that. All he knew was that outside that dungeon was a world that was upside down.

It was on the fifth or sixth day of being in the dungeon, that a German officer arrived to announce that they would be soon boarding a train to their next destination. Talk amongst the men speculated as to their next holding place.

Frank had a feeling that things were about to get worse.

When they were led out of the dungeon the next day, it took a while for Frank's eyes to adjust to the sunlight. They were escorted across the torn and wrecked town streets to the train depot. Frank heard one of the officers ask one of the German guards who spoke English where they were going.

"Fallingbostell," was the answer.

Just then, the train that had been moving slowly finally stopped.

A German officer ordered them to line up, which everyone did without protest. Then a pair of soldiers proceeded to walk down the line, handing a paper sack to each man. Frank took his and opened it to find a stick of beef jerky and molding bread.

As the door to one of the boxcars opened, the gloom of the dungeon seemed to reappear. Inside the boxcar were more POWs. With a gesture, the German soldiers ordered them into the boxcar. Someone asked how long it would take till they reached Fallingbostell.

"Two days," was the clipped English reply.

Frank pulled himself up into the boxcar, and the smell of sweat, bodies, and feces overwhelmed him. He almost gagged, but controlled himself.

Two days.

He looked in his paper sack, wondering how that would last two days.

He crouched against the opposing wall and counted the men that were coming in against those already in the car. By the time the last man entered, Frank had counted fifty men.

Sardines in a can, he thought.

The door to the boxcar slammed shut with a metal protest.

Even the Preacher was speechless.

Chapter 11
Misery

It was the shit smell that got to him first. They were only about four hours into this ride. Frank tried to ignore it when he first got onto the train car, but the jostling of the men behind him pushed him this way and that.

Before he could really force himself to stay still, he found himself at what could be called the tail end of the car. Next to him was, well, for lack of a better term, the "shithole." It was literally a hole that had been cut out of the steel flooring of the cattle car. It maybe two feet wide in diameter. The sides of it were stained and smeared with dried human feces. And it stank.

Not to mention that there was freezing cold air that whistled through the hole and chilled Frank through his Polish woolen overcoat that had been issued to him and all the POWs before they boarded the train.

Frank shivered and tried to hold his breath for the ten thousandth time.

Clickity–Clack

Clickity–Clack

The train's wheels ate up the steel mileage with a steady staccato beat. It had already assumed a kind of background noise in Frank's head. Then there were the coughing, gagging noises of the men next to him.

Everyone had found a place to sit, with some lining the walls to the metal car and the rest in the middle, knees pulled to their chests, back–to–back.

Clickity–Clack

Clickity–Clack

Frank, when he realized that he had wound up next to "the hole" he tried to negotiate his way away from it. But he couldn't do it. There just wasn't room.

"Excuse me," Frank heard a familiar voice, it sounded like Preacher's, "Wanna swap?"

Frank looked in the direction of the voice, and sure enough, Preacher was negotiating his way down the line of men against the wall toward him.

Oh God! What is he up to? Frank thought.

Seeing as how Preacher was moving *toward* the "hole" and they had a chance to move *away,* Preacher quickly found himself sitting right next to Frank.

"Whew!" Preacher waved his hand in front of his nose, "That stinks!"

"Tell me something I don't know," grumbled Frank.

Just then, one of the men who was standing about two feet away, moved quietly over to the "hole", unbuckled his pants, let them drop to his ankles, and squatted.

"Oh God!" Frank moaned, "Kill me now!"

Preacher turned his head to the side, and covered his mouth and nose. Frank didn't have enough time to do that. His stomach twisted on him violently and he began retching and dry heaving between his knees.

The man who was doing his business was a study in complete and total focus on a rust stain on the cattle–car wall. He acted oblivious to Frank, Preacher, and everyone else in the room.

Frank could only think to himself, *when you gotta go...you gotta go...but damn! This stinks!*

A moment later, but it seemed an eternity to Frank, the man pulled up his pants, buckled them, and moved back to the center of the car. As he moved away, Frank heard him mumble, "Sorry man...sorry."

Frank nodded in acknowledgment. He understood. He didn't like it. But he understood.

Trying to distract himself, he looked at Preacher and said, "Why did you do that? Move down here with me?"

Preacher returned his look with a shrug of his shoulders, "I dunno, Battle, cause misery loves company, I guess."

"You mean you're miserable? You?"

"Hey..." Preacher explained, "Let's just say that I'm a guy who doesn't like to see someone suffer alone..."

"Suffer?"

Preacher looked him dead in the eye, and with as dead–level a voice as possible said, "Frank...you're next to a shithole...you're going to become intimate with just about every man's ass over the next two days...yeah, I'd say you're headed for Miserableville."

Frank groaned.

Four hours turned into six, then eight, then twelve...

As night came upon them, someone, Frank wasn't sure who, had made the suggestion that everyone should sleep in two hour rotations. So every two hours, half the men moved to one end of the car and laid down as best they could, while everyone else stood at the other end of the car. Every two hours, they switched.

Sleep and stand.

Clickity–clack

Sleep and stand.

Clickity–clack

Frank reached into his paper sack and withdrew the molding bread. He tore a small hunk off and put it in his mouth. The texture of the bread was overwhelmingly nullified by the stench next to him.

In the twelve hours that they had been riding in this cattle–car, the body heat from fifty men had actually turned it into a sweatbox. Frank was sweating and freezing at the same time. The cold air that roared through the "hole" had managed to seep into his coat and clothes, freezing the sweat that coated his flesh.

In addition, the body heat had somehow mingled with the smell and created a kind of super–scent. This vapor was so thick that it filled the spaces between the men, like a miasma. It seeped into the Polish overcoats and settled in like a tick in shaggy dog's hide. Frank could swear that in the dim light, he could slice the miasma with his hand, and actually *see* it.

It was a relief, the next day, when the train actually stopped and they were allowed to step outside into the winter cold. Frank didn't know which was the more pleasurable, the chance to stretch his legs and walk around, or the crisp winter air that purged the stench of the car from his nose.

They stopped long enough for all the men in all the cars to relieve themselves and grab a breath of fresh air before they were forced back into the giant tin cans that stank of sweat and feces. This happened four or five times a day that second day. Sometimes, they stood in the cold for over two to four hours. One of the men was brave enough to ask a Kraut who spoke a little English why they were stopping.

"Other trains. Important."

From that, they deduced that their train was not a priority in the transportation routes. Obviously, they had been shunted to the side while more important trains came and went, passing by them like giant rushing metal millipedes on roller skates. That thought, as crazy as it was, actually made Frank break open a brief smile as he sat on a fallen log, watching the train pass.

It's funny how the craziest thoughts can make you smile.

By the end of the second day, the smile was definitely gone as Frank chewed on the last of his beef jerky and molded bread.

The third day brought with it an expectation that their journey was about to end.

It didn't.

Again, three or four times, the men found themselves sidelined by the priority trains used to contribute to the German war effort. It got to the point where Frank was willing to endure the hell of the boxcar over the long waits, if to only speed up the journey to wherever they were headed.

The men around him, including Preacher, who was no longer chatty, or even cheerful, echoed his thoughts. The misery was etched on the lines of his face, just like every other man in that tin can.

By the end of the third day, the only sound that seemed louder than the clickity–clack, was the collective roar in their stomachs. Sour faces and constrained tempers were the norm. Even though they were all in this together, tempers were short, and civility was raw and unkempt.

No one spoke.

No one told jokes.

No one complained.

They just endured.

Night fell.

Sleep and stand

Clickity–clack

Sleep and stand

Clickity–clack

The third night turned into a fourth day of sweat, feces, and silent teeth–grinding endurance. After the second stopover, waiting for priority trains to pass, someone was brave enough to ask the same German guard the most pressing question.

"How much longer?"

"Almost there," he answered in a tone that was lacking in any assurance or believability.

Back on the car.

Clickity–clack

Clickity–clack

Frank's mind was so dulled, that he couldn't even daydream. He hadn't had any amount of proper sleep, so he simply existed in the hellish moment for what it was. Surrounded by the stench, the cold metal, the miasma, and coated with a disgusting sweat that froze him, Frank wondered if he weren't already dead.

What if I'm dead and this is hell?

When the train stopped some undetermined time later, the boxcar door was swung open, and the men were greeted with a new, and most welcome sight.

A train yard.

They had arrived.

The hell was over.

At least for this night.

Chapter 12
Silent Night Holy Night

It was nighttime, December 20, when they were unceremoniously loaded like cattle onto another train car. At Fallinbostell, also known as Stalag 11B, there were more German soldiers to go around, and more train cars to use, so thirteen men, including Frank, Preacher and the Judge, found themselves on one end of cattle–car with clean straw on the floor, separated by a fence from five soldiers armed with burp guns.

The stay in Fallinbostell had been brief, but welcome after the hell that they endured getting there. Everyone's mood had picked up a tiny bit after they had arrived. At least until they were informed that there were more miles to cover.

As Frank, Judge, and Preacher lifted themselves into the cattle car, the smell of fresh hay was a welcome and surprising sensation. It was just enough to soften the hard floor of the car and made it just a little easier to sleep upon that night. The first night passed without many words between anyone. The Germans kept to their side and the prisoners to theirs.

December 21 brought a cold morning, but Frank awoke, having slept a little better than he had in days. The train stopped a few times, pulling over to a side track so other trains with a higher priority would pass. It was during one of those long waits that Preacher approached Frank quietly.

"Boy...Frank, that was hell wasn't it?"

Frank studied Preacher's face. There were lines that had appeared in the young man's profile. He didn't look so young anymore. Frank doubted any of them did.

"Yeah, Preacher. It was."

Frank didn't feel like talking.

Preacher didn't seem to notice, "Where do you think we're goin'?"

Frank shrugged his shoulders, "I dunno. Wherever it is, it sure is taking too damn long to get there."

"Yeah," Preacher agreed.

There was a moment of awkward silence between the two of them as the priority train careened down the tracks only fifty feet away. Preacher stared at the tracks as they bounced under the strain of the tons of metal. He wanted to say something, Frank could feel it, but the boy was too scared to.

"What is it, Preacher?"

Preacher looked up at him, a genuine expression of fear stalked his eyes, "Are we going to make it, Frank? I mean..."

Frank spit out a piece of straw that he had been chewing on absently, "Preacher, you can't think like that."

"But...Frank, there's no telling where..."

"Preacher..." Frank's hardened his voice just a bit to catch the man's attention, "Stop. Just stop. Those kinds of thoughts are going to kill you. Do you understand?"

Preacher nodded slightly, like he heard Frank, but fear was still stark in his eyes.

"Look, Preacher," Frank continued, "I've gotten to the point where I don't think about tomorrow anymore. I can't. It's too depressing. Tomorrow's not guaranteed. Is it? Is it?"

Preacher shook his head.

"To tell you the truth, man, I'm just as scared as you. But you can't let that be who you are. You're more than fear. You're a United States Army Officer, for Pete's sake! Remember that! Remember your training! Don't think about what might happen! You'll make yourself sick! What happened to that man that I first met, huh? What happened to the Preacher? Where did he go? He was full of confidence and hope!"

Preacher looked down at the ground, finally listening to Frank's words.

Frank leaned in, his voice dropping, "Don't let them kill your spirit, man. It's all you got left! And we need everyone...I mean everyone...to make it home...okay?"

Preacher nodded, his eyes still on the ground.

A Guard shouted for them to return to the cattle car.

Frank walked to the car, realizing he needed to hear those words from himself as much as Preacher did. Somewhere in the back of his mind, he heard The Wolf chuckling.

One thing that actually made the situation a little better, was the fact that there was a window in the train car. Frank could actually see where they had gone and were going. Many of the men would swap out the position across from the window, just so everyone got a chance to look outside and feel a bit better. The unknown was more terrifying than anything they could imagine.

The second thing that made their situation better was the German guards' attitudes. During the second day of this journey, they seemed to relax around the POWs. At some point during the day, the guards took down the fence that divided the car. They still held their guns close, but their faces and postures spoke of a respect for them that Frank had not seen before. Before long, they were speaking in broken English to some of the men in quiet conversations, even sharing a joke or two.

Frank knew that none of the prisoners had any illusions about escape at this point. They were, for all practical purposes, lost in Germany. Even if they were to escape, they couldn't speak the language. So many of the men simply made the best out the situation. By the end of the second day, spirits were higher than they had been in several weeks.

December 22 brought with it a morning of relaxed spirits and eagerness to see where they had traveled through the night. As Frank looked out the window of the car, he saw a city devastated.

Houses stood, blackened and gutted by the fires that burned them to skeletal remains. Streets were no longer smooth, but pitted and pockmarked by the gaping concrete holes left from bombs. Cars were overturned or crushed by other cars that had been flipped from the explosions that had blanketed the city. Towers stood at precarious angles, ready to topple. Some apartment buildings had their outer walls ripped clean from them, exposing their rooms to the outside like a dream of finding yourself at work in your underwear. Everyone could see you for what you really were. Everyone could see into these apartments and know how their occupants really lived. It was almost embarrassing to look at.

It was shocking.

It was breath–taking.

It was sobering.

"Where?" was one man's half–spoken question before another man answered it quickly.

"Berlin, see the signs?" He indicated with a finger the twisted signs with German written on it, with the city's name prominent.

"Aw man…" said another, "I never…" he didn't finish that statement.

Every set of POW eyes looked toward the Germans. They sat there, faces blank, but the pain was evident. This was their homeland. Their city. And they had the guns right now.

At that moment, no one dared to even breathe the wrong way.

But the Germans didn't put the fence back up. They didn't have scowls of anger on their faces. There appeared only room for sadness.

Finally, the train slowed and came to a stop.

A German left the train car, obviously to get orders.

They were parked in a train yard.

The guard returned, spoke to his fellow soldiers, and they all nodded.

One of them who spoke with broken English, tried to explain that this group of thirteen was to be escorted to a food line and asked for there to be no trouble.

All of the POWs nodded their head in understanding and compliance.

Frank, Preacher, and Judge followed the rest of the men, guided by the Germans away from the train yard and down some deserted streets. They picked their way past blasted craters, burned husks of metal that resembled cars, and shells of buildings that were once whole and unblemished by ash and soot.

Finally, they came to a gathering of people: soldiers mostly, but some groups were obviously other POWs. They were escorted to a particular line, and Frank noted how respectful the soldiers were. There was no, from what he could tell, name–calling or cursing at them. No provocative looks or gestures from any of the soldiers. All was orderly and precise.

Frank received a metal bowl of soup, a cup of water, and a slice of bread. He followed his group to a row of picnic tables cordoned off from other tables. Their guards from the train sat next to them, talking amongst themselves, but they showed no real concern about Frank's group. Oh sure, they held their guns at the ready the whole time, but Frank could feel the relaxed air around them.

There was no real conversation at the picnic tables. Not with the Germans sitting with them, despite their relaxed postures. No one was sure if one of them didn't actually speak English well and was listening for any information they could pass onto their superiors. So the conversation was practically non–existent.

Frank did take his time with his soup though. He recognized this as one of those moments where he could savor the little that life had come to offer him. Hot soup on a cold winter day. Nothing could beat that.

Except Freedom.

When all the men had finished their soup, Frank assumed they would be corralled back to the train. Instead, the Germans simply kept them there. They gave no explanations.

Explanations? Hell, it's their show, Frank thought, *they don't do explanations.*

Finally, a lone soldier approached their table, saluted the commanding officer, and spoke to him in a hushed tone. The next moment, the Germans were motioning for Frank and the others to get up and start moving.

The short walk back through the ruined streets gave Frank another clear understanding of how bad war was.

It wasn't good.

It wasn't noble.

It wasn't constructive.

It was hell on Earth.

It birthed ash, soot, twisted metal, decaying flesh, hunger, and grief. It was the sum of all things bad in the world. Frank glanced at the German walking a few feet to his right, his burp gun at the ready.

War was the sum of all things bad, he told himself, and these guys had started it. As chummy as they were with him and the other prisoners, Frank reminded himself that these were the bad guys.

War was hell, but, as Frank reflected on it, the Germans had made it necessary for them to take part in it.

They reached their train car, only to find that it had been switched to another train. Frank noticed, as did the other men, that one of the German guards wasn't with them. There were now four instead of five. One of them was missing.

As Frank lifted himself into the car, he saw that the Germans had something new sitting on one of the benches.

A cake.

A chocolate cake.

As they moved back into their section of the car, Frank watched the Germans. None of the guards paid any attention to the cake.

It must belong to the guard who is missing, Frank thought.

Frank eyed the cake, sitting undisturbed and alone on the bench. None of the German guards paid attention as he casually walked up and sat next it. Frank sat there for an hour, staring out the window. When he moved toward the back of the car again, none of the guards noticed that the cake went with him.

Night fell, and the sound of the metal wheels carried with them a hypnotic rhythm. Frank sat at the very back of the car. Most of the Germans had gone to sleep, with the exception of one, who sat reading a paperback that he had kept in one of his overcoat pockets. Frank wondered what kind of paperback it was.

Next to him sat Preacher, whose spirit was coming back. He still looked like they all did, lean and hungry, worry–lines across his face, but the sparkle was back in his eye.

"You know Frank," he said as he spoke around the mouthful of stolen chocolate cake, "I think that God knows what is going on."

"What are you talking about?"

"Okay...so I got to thinking about that question you asked me, remember?"

Frank nodded, remembering that he had asked how could a loving God permit such evil to occur.

"And then we had that hellacious trip, right?"

"Yeah, what of it?"

"Well...look at us now, we are, more or less, in a better place than we have been in, right?"

Frank nodded, chewing on another piece of the stolen cake.

"All I'm saying is that when we ask the question, 'Why does God allow bad things to happen' I think we're really saying that we think He doesn't know about what's going on. But the truth of the matter is this..." Preacher held up a finger to make his point, "He does know what's going on, and we are the ones responsible for our actions. For our response to the evil and bad things around us. We are responsible to stop the bad things from happening."

"So," Frank replied, "what you're saying is that we are responsible to stop the bad things from happening."

"Right!" Preacher nodded.

"So bad things happen, and we are responsible for how we respond to them."

"Yep," he said between mouthfuls, "I think our response to evil is one of the ways that we will be judged by Him in the end."

"What about this cake?" asked the Judge, who had been listening silently across from Frank. He chewed on his piece thoughtfully.

Preacher shrugged, "Hey! It's cake! What can you say spiritually about cake? I don't know."

"Damn good cake," said another man, Frank thought his name was Hendricks.

"Yeah," Frank stared out the window into the cold German night air, the moon a giant silver platter hung in the night sky, "damn good cake."

The 23rd of December was another day of travel, and judging by the scenery, one of the men guessed that they were in Poland. They were only diverted twice that day, to allow other priority trains to pass. The German soldiers were oblivious to the fact that they were missing a chocolate cake. Or perhaps they just didn't care.

There was little conversation on that day.

Frank thought that everyone was ready for the train ride to be over. He knew he was. He figured they were headed for a POW camp. Frank wondered what the camp would be like.

The day passed without event.

The 24th of December came with an announcement by one of the guards that they would be arriving at their destination at the end of the day. There was visible restlessness on everyone's faces.

The train wasn't diverted at all that day.

The metal wheels beneath them ate up the miles in a staccato beat.

It wasn't until someone asked what the date was, that Frank realized that it was Christmas Eve.

But he wasn't the only one.

Frank wasn't particularly religious, he could admit that, but he had a certain reverence for Christmas. So he wasn't put off when the singing started.

It was Preacher who did it.

One moment he was quiet, lost in his thoughts. The next, he was singing softly to himself.

"Silent Night...Holy Night..."

Frank knew that one.

As did all the other men.

To their surprise, so did the Germans.

Before long, the entire car was a chorus of Christmas carols.

Germans and Americans.

There may have been a language barrier, but those songs transcended it. The Peace of Christmas Eve took over the atmosphere of the train.

Frank saw smiles on the Germans faces as they sang. He saw smiles on the faces of the men with him. There might have even been a smile on his face as well.

He didn't know how long the singing lasted, but when the train stopped that night, they exited the car with a sense of relief, reverence, and peace. No matter what came, tomorrow was about the King of Peace coming into the world.

Now if only the world would pay attention and stick to it.

Chapter 13
The Velvet Prison

They arrived at Oflag 64, Zubin, Poland, at about 9 o'clock at night. The snow had stopped falling, but the ground was covered with white powder. They were escorted from the train yard to Oflag 64's entrance.

After a few formalities, they were taken to the office of a captain, who turned out to be the adjutant of the camp. The man reached into his desk and withdrew several packs of cigarettes. Tossing them onto the desk, he said, "Help yourself, gentlemen. I'm Captain Burns. Welcome to Oflag 64."

"What is this place?" asked one of the new arrivals.

"It's a boys' boarding school. Although Germans and barbed wire surround us, this is an American camp. We run this place like any American military instillation back home. Our Senior American Officer, SAO, is Colonel Paul Goode. Some of the men call him 'Pop Goode,' because he takes care of us. You'll meet him soon enough. He's got five Lieutenant Colonels, a Major, and me. Plenty of senior staff to go around."

An aide appeared with an armful of paper and pencils at the door.

Captain Burns noticed him and said, "For now, boys, the first thing I need you to do is fill out these registration forms. We need your name, rank, serial number, outfit, college, and home town. We're going to be posting this information in the camp ASAP."

"Why is that?" someone asked.

Captain Burns held up two fingers, "Two reasons: First, to keep an accurate record of all POWs. Second, whenever a list of new POWs is posted, everyone at the camp checks it out to see if they know anyone. This prevents the Krauts from slipping spies into the camp."

"How does that work?" another man asked.

"Simple," grunted Captain Burns, "If there is someone here who recognizes you and can vouch for your identity, then you are good to go. If not, well...we'll take care of things."

He had already noticed a complete change in his sense of safety. A knot that had formed at the back of his neck began to loosen. He hadn't been aware of it at all.

This is a safe place, he thought to himself. *I'm finally in a safe place.*

It was a change, to be sure, from the hell they had been through up to this point. For that, Frank was grateful.

All in all, Frank thought to himself, *this is a hell of a lot better than what we came from. But I'm still in a Velvet Prison.*

All he had to do was to look out the windows at the Guard Towers and barbed wire to see that.

The next morning, while he was eating breakfast in the cafeteria, a familiar face sat down across from him with a smile of recognition. It took just a moment for the man's name to surface: Herb Hayes.

"Herb?" Frank asked.

Herb's smile broke into a beaming gusher of a grin, "Frank! You're here! It's so good to see you! I mean, this is a POW camp, but...Man! You're alive! This is great!"

Frank couldn't help but smile in return. He had gone to high school with Herb and actually worked at the same job with him for a while. This was a welcome sight. They spoke briefly about their individual experiences that had led them to Oflag 64.

"Does this mean I'm cleared?" Frank asked.

Herb nodded his head, "Yep! You are the one and only Frank Battle that I know! Couldn't be anyone else as far as I'm concerned!"

"So what do you do around here?" Frank asked.

Herb held up his gloved hands and wiggled his fingers, "I play bridge! You should join me. I personally think that it is the best way to pass the time in here."

"I might just do that," Frank replied. He shivered from the cold, "Is there anywhere I can get a pair of those?" He nodded toward the woolen gloves.

"Sure! I know just who to get them from...He's due to come in today anyway."

"Who is it?"

"We call him, 'The Swede.' He's from Sweden. He is an international representative of the YMCA and the Salvation Army. He visits every three to four months, bringing with him books, blankets, coats, paper, pencils, and anything else the Krauts let him bring in. He's a real Godsend around here. Seeing as today is Christmas, he should arrive today. I'll get you a pair of gloves and an extra blanket."

"Thanks Herb," Frank was suddenly moved by this strange circumstance. It seemed too convenient, an old friend finding him here, in the middle of a POW camp in Poland, some thousands of miles from home. He felt something flutter in his stomach, and he tried to push it down.

"You okay?" asked Herb.

"Yeah," Frank waved a hand at him, "just trying to get used to everything. I'm fine." The truth was, that Frank felt something like tears trying to bubble up from deep inside, tears of relief, tears of frustration, tears of gratitude. But this wasn't the place. It wasn't a safe place. So Frank clamped down on those feelings and buried them...deep.

Herb didn't seem to notice, "Okay, Frank, I'll get back to you later today with your gloves...see ya." He held out his hand for Frank to shake. Frank did, noticing the man's strong grip.

Sure enough, Herb was true to his word, and by the end of the day, Frank was wearing his new woolen gloves and playing his sixth hand of bridge. There was the sound of music in the air. The Swede had brought music instruments with him, and several of the officers knew how to play. The sounds of big band and a bit of jazz echoed down the halls from one of the rooms that had been designated the "Music Hall."

As the days passed, Frank quickly fell into a routine. The Geneva Convention forbade any officers having to work, and there were about fifty or so POWs who were enlisted men who actually did all the main work in the camp. Frank learned that there were about fifteen hundred US officers kept at Oflag 64. He spent most of his time, at least six hours of it, playing bridge with gloves on. Frank attended a small church service that was held by some of the men who had been pastors before enlisting. He found Preacher had settled right in with those guys. He also attended the regular music shows that musical officers produced every two or three days after rehearsing. But most of his time was spent playing bridge, which he came to enjoy immensely.

Every man was given a Red Cross parcel, and Frank would surrender some of the contents to the cooks, where they took the Klim, which was powdered milk, the instant coffee, and tin of meat. The kitchen would take the meat out of the boxes, and use it as the basis to feed all the Kriegies in the Mess Hall. The Kriegies also had an inventive way of using the Red Cross milk cans and combining them to create smokeless heaters, utilizing Klim, chocolate, bread, and raisins. The men would use these smokeless heaters to prepare a variety of delicacies to relieve everyone of the monotony of the usual menu of meals.

Periodically, the Germans would send in a "ferret," a German guard, to scout out and inspect the premises.

The first Kriegie that saw him would shout out, *"Goon coming in!"*

All eyes turned toward him. Whatever you were doing, when the Kraut appeared, you dropped what you were doing, and stared him down. Sometimes it worked. Sometimes the Kraut got so nervous will all those eyes watching, that he finished whatever "duty" he was performing so he could get out of there. Other times, the guy had guts of iron, and obviously didn't give a damn who was looking at him.

Evenings were something that Frank began to look forward to, and not just because he could sleep to pass the hours. Once everyone had been cleared by security, a messenger would give a daily report from "The Bird." This was a secret radio that someone had built out of smuggled parts. "The Bird" was tuned to the BBC and from it, Frank and the rest of the men learned of the progress of the Allies. It was nice to finally know what was going on with their side of the war.

Frank also learned of the secret effort to escape. There was an actual Escape Committee he heard about, that was digging a tunnel to the outside. For a while, they used old Red Cross boxes to carry the dirt from the tunnel to the low attics of the barracks. This worked for a while, Frank heard, until the weight of the dirt almost caused the ceiling to break. The Escape Committee then came up with a brilliant idea of sewing small sacks to the inside of the trousers of the men and filling them with dirt. These men would then "go for a walk" on the 10 acres outside, where they would dispose of the dirt without ever being discovered. It worked beautifully, and tons of dirt and debris was removed from the tunnel day–by–day, hour–by–hour.

Frank had just about gotten used to Oflag 64, when word came of a fierce Russian offensive into Poland. It was January 18, during the second "appell," where they checked the roster twice a day to make sure that everyone was in the camp, that it was announced that the entire camp would begin a forced march back into Germany to another camp. The camp members were given just a few hours to prepare.

Red Cross parcels were distributed one last time, one per man, while several groups were organized to construct hastily prepared backpacks to carry extra blankets and supplies for each man to carry. In addition, those Kriegies who didn't smoke, like Frank, had returned their smokes to the Supply Warehouse. When preparations began for the march, the extra cigarettes were passed out to whoever still had cartons or packs that they had not requested. Frank figured that they could be invaluable in the days ahead if they could be used as a trading resource with civilians.

The weather temperature outside at that time, day–to–day, was zero Fahrenheit. There were six inches of snow on the ground. Frank groaned to himself as he sat on his bunk, sewing his backpack together, occasionally looking outside at the falling snow.

"How's it coming, Frank?" asked Preacher, who had dropped by.

"I'm not looking forward to this," Frank replied, gesturing with his chin to the weather outside. "This is going to be bad...real bad. I can feel it."

Preacher squinted his eyes at the falling snow outside, "Yeah, it's like the train all over again, isn't it?"

Frank could only nod his head as he turned his attention back to his sewing.

"I try not to think about that..." he finally said, still sewing.

"Yeah," agreed Preacher, "It's probably best if we don't. I guess we've got to keep our spirits up somehow. I dunno of any other way that we are going to make it."

"Look, Preacher, you're all chummy with those priests–types...why don't you get them to have a final service for us? Before we start the march? Something to encourage us? What do you think?"

There was a gleam in Preacher's eyes, "I think that's a grand idea, Frank. A grand idea indeed! I'll talk to the others about it."

With that said, Preacher left, suddenly on a mission.

Frank smiled to himself. Sometimes, he felt too smart for his own good.

It was announced that there would be a final church service for all those Kriegies who would like to attend.

The next morning, at nine o'clock, all the officers stood in the yard during appell, ready to march.

However, there was a slight snag in the Germans' plans. There were about twenty Kriegies who were missing.

The truth was, that the Escape Committee had been given the go–ahead to hide themselves in the tunnel they had constructed. So Frank and the remainder of the POWs stood in the falling snow for two hours, while the Germans searched and searched the premises for the missing Americans. Finally, the order was given to march. Frank started off with a slight smile on his face as he looked at the German guards wearing faces of confusion and frustration.

It was a small victory, and even though he wasn't a part of the group that remained hidden and was soon to be free, he was part of the side that gave the Krauts a black eye after all.

The camp Commandant advised Colonel Goode that their march would be sixty miles west to Stettin. With that, all the Kriegies groaned. Who can walk sixty miles?

But twenty of them didn't have to.

And that felt good to Frank.

Despite the numbness in his toes.
Despite his shivering in zero temperatures.
Despite the sixty–odd miles ahead of them.
Frank felt good.
He tried to hold onto that feeling as long as he could.

Chapter 14
Hellmarch (Part 1)

Day One

There is one good thing about the walking, Frank realized as the long column of POWs moved like a giant sinuous snake through the snow–covered roads of Poland. *At least it means you're alive. I'm alive.*

Night was starting to come over them, as the snow continued its silent and implacable smothering of everything in sight. There was, for a time, brief conversation between men as they marched.

However, the ice and snow had a way of sucking more than the warmth out of your body, Frank noted. It also stole your thoughts and numbed your memory. From time to time, Frank would try to remember earlier events, conversations, or even landscapes that he had seen. But it was all blurred out and lost in this world of white.

There was little sound, except for the wheeze of his own breathing, the crunch of snow under his boots, an occasionally cough or sniffle. Now amplify that by fifteen hundred, and it was the kind of cacophony that anyone could become numb to. Something happened to a man's hearing in those conditions. He would become so focused on himself, and merely putting one foot in front of the other, that he would lose the ability to selectively listen. Many times, Frank found himself startled when someone would call his name or say something, anything, to him.

Did I just hear that? Or am I imagining it? he would ask himself.

Then the speaker would say something again, and Frank would have to concentrate his focus to understand what was actually said.

"What did you say?" was the most frequent thing to come out of his mouth.

He was too cold to talk.

He was too cold to listen.

He was just too cold...period.

Frank kept his eyes down, focused on the ground just in front of him, following the footsteps of the guy in front of him.

Crunch....crunch...crunch...

The sound of fifteen hundred boots in snow was overwhelming.

Crunch...crunch...crunch...

Frank walked with a blank mind...his thoughts as white as the snow that fell.

Crunch....crunch...crunch...

Finally, the boots in front of him stopped. Frank brought his head up, suddenly aware of the change in the monotony of this Hellmarch, as he called it. Up ahead, the word was being passed down. Finally it reached Frank and continued on like a ripple in water.

"Time to rest. Turn in for the night. Pull out your rations for the day. Don't eat too much. Save your strength."

These were the messages that were passed back through the line. Frank's mind was too numb to think too hard about it.

"Hey Frank..." a familiar voice spoke to him from behind.

It took Frank a moment to realize that the voice was addressing him. He turned his head to see one of his friends that he had made, a Lieutenant Dallas Smith, "Smitty", behind him, snow dusting his full–grown beard. They all had beards now. Which was good. Kept the face warm.

"Yeah?" Frank replied.

"Why don't we buddy–up?"

Before the march began, there had been talk of every two men partnering together to ensure survival. It was called the Buddy System, for lack of a better or more elegant phrase. It meant that you shared your food with your buddy. You combined your blankets together and shared them with your buddy so you wouldn't freeze. You basically relied on your buddy, and he on you, to keep you alive.

Frank didn't even have to think about it.

"That's a great idea, Dallas."

Dallas coughed, his breath leaving clouds that evaporated in the zero temperatures. "I thought so too."

Each man was issued their portion of rations, boiled potatoes and thin soup, with black bread. Always black bread.

On this first day, Frank, using a small penknife, sliced the bread they had been issued, and spread a thin layer of margarine on it. Then he held out the two slices to Dallas, who choose which slice he would take. Tomorrow, Dallas would slice the bread, and Frank would choose the slice. This system kept things fair and equitable, so no one would be accused of eating more food than his buddy.

They ate their boiled potatoes, thin soup, which was really nothing more than a substitute soup mix, and the black bread. Then they, along with nine or ten other guys, spent time in front of a small fire, trying to absorb as much heat as possible from it. Finally, their internal clocks told them it was time to sleep, so they turned in.

That night, the first night, Frank and Dallas slept under their shared blankets in a barn loft that was abandoned. The rest of the men had taken up the remaining space in the barn, the farmhouse, and the adjoining farms less than a quarter of a mile away. Using their boots to weigh down the corners of the blankets and trap the heat under it, they slept without dreaming.

Day Three

The entire column of POWs reached a small, unknown, and unremarkable town by the third day. It was deserted.

Surprisingly, they did not march that day.

Someone noticed that the guards were conspicuously absent. It didn't take long to realize that they weren't just absent, they were gone.

Apparently, there was only one lone German officer left in charge of the entire column of fifteen hundred men.

One officer.

Once word got out, it didn't take a rocket scientist to consider the opportunity this presented every single man.

Escape.

This was their chance to get away.

It was common knowledge that the Russians were not that far behind the column. In fact, they could hear the exchange of small arms fire in the distance. For some men, that was all they needed to know.

Five hundred men headed for the hills that day.

Frank and Dallas sat near a fire, and soon found themselves finally warm.

Finally, as expected, Dallas said, "So Frank, what do you want to do?"

The food truck had delivered substitute coffee to all the men, and Frank sipped on his, trying to stay warm. He scratched his beard, thinking.

"If we get separated, Dallas, and I end up by myself, I could very well wind up in a field with a bullet through my back. Where would that leave me? I would be dead and no one to know about it. That would kill my mother. She would never know what happened to me. You know?"

Dallas nodded his head in understanding and agreement.

"I can't do that to my mother, Dallas. I can't do that to my family. I think we'll be better off if we stay here. I don't want to risk it."

Dallas sipped his coffee and said nothing.

But he didn't disagree with Frank.

So they spent the rest of the day, warmed by the fire, watching for the return of the German guards. Frank didn't care if he and Dallas turned out to be the only two men who stayed behind. He wasn't going to be an anonymous corpse that remained undiscovered until spring.

The German guards returned at night. They had been sent back to ambush the attacking Russians. But now they returned to their duties to guard the column.

The next morning, Hellmarch continued, this time with less than a thousand men.

Day Twelve and Day Fifteen

Two incidents happened that were very unusual.

First, one day as they were resting, a boy of about ten, came up to Frank, and said, *"Happen zie seife?"*

One of the other Kriegies said, "He wants to know if you have any soap, Battle."

Frank nodded his head, "Yes, I do."

The boy reached in his pocket and pulled out a handful of onions, indicating that he wanted soap for onions. Frank happened to have a bar of Ivory soap in his knapsack, and he traded for the onions. Then, the boy produced another handful of onions out of his other pocket, most likely in gratitude for the trade.

It wasn't until that night, when they were ready to eat their potatoes, and they inserted the onions with the potatoes, that they realized how much better the potatoes were with the onions.

Another incident occurred as the column was walking through a very small town. The local citizens realized that they were Americans. Immediately, they became very excited and invited them to come into their homes. Within minutes, the column disappeared and the Germans were apoplectic trying to collect them and get them back into the streets. Frank ran down a side street, at the end of which, two elderly women were waving at him. He ran into their house, and they embraced him lustily saying, *"Amerikanish coom!"* They offered him a loaf of bread, so he reached in his pocket and handed them a pack of cigarettes, whereupon they offered him another loaf of bread. Once again, they hugged each other, and Frank ran back up the street to rejoin the column.

Day Sixteen

Two weeks.

That was how long they were told this march would last.

Two weeks.

Each day was at least fifteen to twenty kilometers of a march in the dead of the Polish winter. Frank wondered, for the umpteenth time, if the Germans were trying to kill them just by exposure to the elements. If the prisoners all died, how could their guards stand trial for war crimes? They could just blame it on the weather? Right?

A raging winter storm howled outside a deserted music hall, where the prisoners huddled together. This was supposed to be the end of their 60–mile march to their destination of Stettin. Instead, they had been re–routed. Now they were on the way toward the Baltic Sea. The Russians, even though they were less than a mile away, were anxious to get to the Oder River, where Stettin was located. North of Stettin, the Oder Estuary branched out in numerous tributaries that made it impossible for an army to proceed. The Germans, recognizing that, turned the column ninety degrees north, and headed for the Baltic Sea.

The Kriegie column was quickly dwindling. Many of the men had gotten sick. As a result, twice, the Germans sent the sick men to the nearest train depot to be shipped to the nearest German facility, Dachau, for treatment. Many times, Frank wondered if those men would ever make it home again.

Now, they were in the midst of another snowstorm from hell. The Germans had realized that they would lose valuable leverage if all of their officers died from exposure, so every time there was an indication of a storm coming, they would shelter their prisoners in nearby churches, barns, schools, and libraries, and this time, a music hall: any structure that could provide them with shelter from the elements served their purpose. Nevertheless, men continued to sicken and get worse from the flu, to hypothermia, to frostbite.

Frank sat down with his back against a wooden partition. Across from him was Dallas. The building they were in was crammed with about seven hundred men remaining from the original fifteen hundred that started this journey. Fortunately, this was the largest building in this medium sized, unnamed town. Several men were already asleep, sprawled out on the stage. Men slept in the theatre seats and the rows of aisles.

There was one thing that helped pass the time for Frank and Dallas when they were cooped up in a place like this. Dallas had managed to smuggle a deck of cards out of Oflag 64. Well, not really smuggle. Nobody cared what small items they took for themselves.

So in the faint light of the few oil lamps positioned high above, Frank and Dallas played a game of Blackjack.

Dallas was the bank. (Not that there was any money to be had, but someone had to be the bank)

He dealt a card.

Frank – a seven

Dallas – a ten

"So…" Dallas said in that low tone that indicated he wanted to have a conversation, "How's the family?"

Frank – an eight

Dallas – a nine. Winner

Frank smiled, they had done this one before, "Well…" he started, and "You know my Mom's got fat ankles My Dad's got gout. But they both still like to dance. So every Friday night, they go out dancing, and then pay for it Saturday morning. So you know what that means…"

Frank – a three

Dallas – a queen

"You have to do the chores…" answered Dallas.

Frank smiled, "Yep…chores it is. I've got to shovel the walk, put salt on the drive, wrestle with the black behemoth in the basement."

Frank – a ten

Dallas – a six

Frank: "Hit me…"

Frank – a five

Dallas – a ten. Busted

"Oh? You have a black behemoth too?" queried Dallas, feigning surprise.

"Oh yes, my Dad loves his black behemoth. Oh sure, it puts out the heat you want, but it's a finicky kind of contraption."

Frank – a Jack

Dallas – a two

Dallas smiled, "And your love life?"

"Oh…you know me…I've got a girl at every port in the world."

Frank – an Ace. Blackjack

"Yeah, that's the Frank Battle I know."

"Yeah, I've got the women coming out of the woodwork for me."

"I'm sure you do…"

Frank – a two

Dallas – an eight

"So…how much longer do you think we'll be?"

Frank – a seven

Dallas – a two

"Hit me…I dunno…word has it that we're going to be crossing into Germany in the next couple of days. From the landscape, I'd say we're headed across the Oder Estuary."

Frank – a five

Dallas – an eight

"You sure are good with maps...how do you do that?"

Frank shrugged, "I dunno...I've been told I have an exact memory. I just remember the things I look at. On the way over here, I studied all the maps that we had of Germany and her borders. I recognized the words on the signs as matching what I read on the maps. Oder Estuary will prevent the Russians from following us...pretty smart if you ask me...Hit me..."

Frank – a four

Dallas – a four– Busted

"Or desperate," Dallas mused, "They must be real desperate to want to hold onto us. Bargaining pieces if you ask me..."

Frank nodded in agreement. "Yeah...that makes sense."

The game continued into the night, as did their speculations on what their future held. When the oil in the lamp finally burned out, Frank and Dallas turned in.

Frank's sleep was dreamless. They had been for quite some time.

Outside, the snowstorm raged mercilessly.

Day Thirty

They crossed into Germany two days later, after crossing the Oder Estuary. The day was clear, with not a cloud in the sky. It would be a good day to get where they were going. Make up for lost time during the snowstorms.

A couple of miles into Germany, while they all stopped at a farm for a short break, Frank found a metal water pump in the yard. He seized the metal handle with a gloved hand, the woolen mitts barely holding back the cold the iron handle radiated. He was sure if he wasn't wearing gloves, in this temperature, the slightest amount of water would freeze his hand to the pump. He worked the pump handle vigorously for a few moments until water, crisp and freezing, burst from the spout.

Leaning down, he drank deeply.

Chapter 15
Hellmarch (Part Two)

Night Thirty–one
Frank lay under his blankets, his back to Dallas' back. They were now in a massive Boy Scout campsite that held several buildings with bunks and toilets. The snow had returned with a vengeance about midway through the day. He was trying to relax, but his stomach was in knots, twisted and cramping.

Oh God, he prayed, *don't let me be one of the sick ones.*

His stomach turned on him in cramped response.

He lay there, barely on the edge of sleep, hoping that his worst fear was not coming true.

Day Thirty–two
Hellmarch worsened.

The next day, Frank found himself having the runs. He squatted at least seven to eight times that day. In the freezing weather, he began to sweat with a fever.

He racked his brains, trying to figure out what could have gotten him sick.

Then...halfway through the day...it came to him in a blinding flash of realization.

The water.

He had been warned by his CO to not drink the native water. His body didn't have the immunities to the bacteria in the water that the Europeans did. Now his body was probably raging with a disease that made his insides turn to mush, and stomach to lead a full–scale rebellion.

Oh God! Not now...Not this! He prayed as feverishly as he felt.

There was no answer.

No burning bush.

No angelic messenger.

Not even a disembodied voice in his head.

Nothing.

It seemed to Frank that God must have missed his phone call.

That, or He really didn't care to begin with.

He and Dallas had found themselves at the rear of the march, due to his frequent stops, which irritated the guards to no end. Several times, he heard a German guard muttering under his breath. Of course, he couldn't make out what was being said, but Frank assumed it was some complaint about the "sick Americans."

"Come on, Frank," said Dallas, helping him back into the marching column, "Hold on, man, hold on."

"I'm trying," Frank replied, "I'm trying."

Day Thirty–nine

A week had passed. In that week, Frank was sure he had lost at least twelve pounds of body weight. He was certain that he had dysentery. It was causing him to defecate at least seven to eight times a day.

During that time, they passed through more small towns, farming communities, and a few large towns. The snow continued to fall, uncon-cerned about Frank's plight, or any of the other men in the Hellmarch. At least two hundred more men had been rerouted to other German camps because they had become too sick to continue the march.

Frank held on.

It was the support of the other men who helped him. Especially Dallas.

There was still no idea where they were headed.

The road before them was an icy hell that promised no end in sight.

But Frank continued.

I will not give up.

Day Forty

Frank was certain he had lost at least twenty–five to thirty pounds now. The word "weak" didn't come anywhere close to describing how he felt. At one point, Colonel Goode came by to check on him.

They were stopped at a small town where there was a train depot. Frank watched as some of those who couldn't go on were being escorted onto a train car. It was just a metal box, with a tarp over the top of it.

"Battle," said Goode, "You can go if you need to. You don't have to stay with us. You're in bad shape. Don't keep doing this to yourself."

Frank took a long look at the train car.

"Colonel," he replied, "If I get in that metal box over there, I might not come out. No...I'll stay with the column."

"Very well." Goode answered, and then paused, "You're a tough man...one of the toughest I've seen."

Frank waved a dismissing hand at him, "I'm not tough, Colonel, I just don't want to die. There's nothing tough about that."

Goode nodded his head and left.

Frank continued to sit there, staring at the dead men who were lifting themselves into that metal box. Despite the fact that he was already cold, Frank shivered with a feeling that went all the way down his spine.

Day Forty–one

It was two days later, when Frank decided that there was a God, after all. The Hellmarch continued, amidst a light falling snow, through a small German community. If Frank had actually had a mind to care about his surroundings, he would have thought it a quaint little town.

This one was populated with Germans, going through their daily business, despite the war that raged all around them. Frank didn't pay attention to them. He just focused on two things: the road and his insides.

"Hey!" someone said loudly, "Look at that!"

Frank ignored him.

Then Dallas said, "Frank, I think you want to see this."

Frank lifted his eyes and followed where Dallas' gloved finger pointed. His vision came to rest upon a German sleigh, being pulled by a packhorse. Frank looked at the sleigh driver, an elderly man of perhaps fifty or so. Nothing remarkable about that.

"What?" he asked, "I don't see…"

Then he *did* see…

The sleigh was packed with Red Cross parcels.

Frank knew immediately what that meant. His heart began to beat faster. He straightened up. "Do they know?" he asked Dallas, "Does the Colonel know?"

"I don't know," answered Dallas.

Ten minutes later, the word came back to them.

The Colonel knew. He demanded that the Germans take them to the Red Cross outpost where they could get the parcels. Frank felt strength, he didn't know where from, return to his limbs.

Perhaps it was the will to live.

An hour later, every two men were given a parcel. Dallas tore open theirs and he asked Frank what he wanted. Frank looked inside the package until he found it.

"Dallas, you can have anything else you want in the box…I want the Kraft cheese,"

Dallas looked at him with confusion on his face.

Frank lifted out the one thing that would save his life and held it in front of Dallas. It was a square of cheese.

Dallas's face broke into a wide grin. Then he took some of the other portions of food and walked away for a while. They had stopped at the outskirts of the town. Frank sat on a frozen stump, eating his cheese. He looked up when Dallas returned.

Dallas had in his arms several more servings of cheese.

The grin on his face never wavered, "I traded for it, Frank. You're going to make it."

"Bless you, Dallas. You're a good man," Frank almost felt like tearing up, and his voice nearly cracked with emotion. But this wasn't the place.

The cheese did its job and stopped Frank's dysentery, saving his life.

Day Forty–two

By everyone's count, they had been on the road for forty–two days. They had traveled nearly five hundred and fifty kilometers, which came somewhere between three hundred and fifty and four hundred miles. When they reached the city of Parchim, there was a train waiting.

Someone asked where they were headed, and a German guard let it slip.

Stalag 13.

Would there be any more marching?

"Nein."

Frank, feeling much better due to ingesting the cheese, sighed with relief. Dallas sat next to him, the same expression on his face.

Hellmarch was over.

Chapter 16
Kingdom of Lice

Hammelburg Germany was the location of Stalag 13B. The final group of men who survived the Hellmarch numbered at about five hundred. They arrived on March 7, 1945. At Stalag 13B, they were joined by a thousand prisoners from the Battle of the Bulge. Then, on top of that, there were three thousand five hundred Serbian POWs. Stalag 13B was, to say the least bursting at the seams.

Somehow, everyone was given a place to bunk. Frank stayed close to Dallas, and in the few days that passed, he developed another friendship with an officer who he came to admire for his attitude and all–around guts, Jay Drake. As Frank began to settle into this new location, which was, on one hand, better than a frozen barn, and on the other hand, worse than Oflag 64, he quickly realized that all the squalor he had been through was nothing compared to the state of Stalag 13B.

"The Kingdom of Lice," is what one officer declared on Frank's second night in the camp. Sure enough, Frank awoke several times throughout the night, feeling lice crawl all over him. He would get up and shake out his shirt and blankets as best he could.

It became a nightly ritual for all men in the camp.

Lice Hour.

Sleeping Lice and Easy.

Do you want a little Lice with your soup?

Frank would pick the lice from his clothes, and lay down, sometimes wishing that he was back in a barn somewhere, even in a frozen ditch. Anywhere where there were no lice.

As crowded as the camp was, order was still maintained. Colonel Goode became the Senior American Officer, in charge of all the men in the camp. He fought for Red Cross parcels, mail, and any other prisoner rights he could find.

The men were housed in hastily constructed wooden bunkhouses. They held enough men to make it crowded, but there was such shoddy workmanship, that cracks in the floors and walls made little protection from the elements. Frank, Dallas, and Jay were fortunately kept together in one bunkhouse.

Most of the day was spent huddled in blankets or around the cast–iron heater that was placed at the center of each bunkhouse. Due to the worsening weather, there was little to nothing to do during the day. Luckily, Dallas held onto his deck of cards, so that provided a small amount of distraction from reality.

One day, after about a week of being there, while Dallas, Jay, and Frank, and a couple of other men played Blackjack, Frank remembered a question he had.

"Anyone know what happened to Preacher? I haven't seen him."

Dallas coughed and shook his head, "I dunno, Frank."

"You mean the Holy Roller?" said a man named Sims, who had survived the Hellmarch with Frank and the others.

"Yeah," Frank said.

"I think he got frostbite on his right foot. Last I remember, he was getting on the train to go get treated."

Frank shuddered, imagining Preacher in that metal box with a canvas tarp over it, freezing as he lost more feeling in his foot. That shouldn't have happened.

Out of all the guys loyal to God and all, that man should have gotten better treatment by the Man Upstairs.

"That's a shame..." Frank was upset, "He's a good guy."

"Yep," agreed Sims, "he had a way of cheering me up when I didn't think I could go on. I dunno how he did it, but he did. Gonna miss him."

"Me too," said Dallas.

"Blackjack," declared Frank.

"Aw...man!" Everyone groaned.

One of the guards called out, "Herr Frank Battle!"

Frank froze upon hearing his name.

What do they want with me?

"Where is Herr Frank Battle?" the German called out in a thick accent.

Frank stood up from his bunk.

"Whaddya want?" he growled.

The German guard looked at him with piercing blue eyes, "Your presence is required at the Commandant's office!"

"Frank you want me to go with you?" Jay asked.

Frank halfway wanted Jay with him, because Jay was a gutsy guy. But he had a feeling he knew what this was about.

"No...I'll be back...I'm sure..."

Jay backed down, and Frank walked up to the guards.

"Lead the way." He nodded with his head toward the outside.

Frank's bunkhouse was situated on the outer row of bunk-houses, close to the gates, so it turned out to be a short walk to the Commandant's office. The falling snow mixed with the frozen mud, making a filthy slush they had to tramp through. In some places, long wooden boards were laid out for the ranking German officers and the Commandant to use without getting their precious boots soiled. Frank was somewhat thankful for those boards that his escorts used now, so he wouldn't have to clean his boots when he returned to the bunkhouse.

But as they made their way across the muck–filled yard, his stomach tightened – he felt worse than he had when he'd had dysentery. There was only one reason he could think of that would explain why he was being summoned.

He entered the building which doubled as the camp office, and noticed that the Commandant was standing outside of his own office, which mean that someone else was occupying it. As the Commandant turned to look at Frank, the expression on his face was at once tight and austere. He called behind him, through the open doorway, to the person who was inside.

"Ahh!" The voice made Frank's insides turn to water, "Herr Battle! Please step inside my office!"

The Wolf.

Frank felt all eyes on him as he walked ever so slowly, feeling like a mouse trapped in a nest of cats, waiting for one of them to pounce on it. Meanwhile, all the cats simply sat there, looking at him, tails swishing, licking their mouths, sniffing the air, and trying to decide when would be the appropriate time to pounce.

Frank entered the office, noticing the large desk and leather–bound chair behind it to his left. In that chair, the Wolf sat, eyes hungry.

"Close the door." The Wolf motioned with a small gesture.

Frank shut the door behind him and stood before the desk.

Even though the Wolf sat while Frank stood, it felt like the man was peering down on him from high up, like Caesar in his gladiator games. The Wolf looked him over meticulously, seeming to read into what he had been through. Finally, after what seemed an hour of scrutiny, he spoke.

"Oflag 64...you survived the march...I'm impressed."

Frank returned the look with a glare of his own, "I'm so pleased that you are impressed. You know, it's been my goal since I signed up to make a good impression on Kraut officers!"

"Still the smart–ass, I see. I would have thought we had rectified that situation by now." The Wolf was smirking.

"Still the sadistic bastard, I see." Frank retorted, "Give me a chance and I'll wipe that smirk off your face!"

"Oh!" The Wolf stood up and walked around the desk, "Herr Battle, there would be nothing more pleasing to me than to allow you that opportunity." His face drew close enough for Frank to smell his breath, foul and hot, "But..." The Wolf placed a leather–gloved finger lightly on Frank's cheek, "the children outside that door would be sooo upset if they didn't get a chance to play...and..." his voice dropped to a whisper, "I have such plans for you! Herr Battle!"

Frank trembled with rage. He clenched his gloved fists. Something... anything...could set him off and then nothing would stop him from choking the life out of The Wolf. Yet, he knew that would mean instant death. He would never get home. He would never see his parents again. He stood there, eyes straight ahead, willing himself to remain in control.

The Wolf walked behind him, his boots creaking on the wooden floor.

Frank shook imperceptibly.

The moment stretched out...two...three...five minutes.

Then...

"You may leave now..." The Wolf pulled open the door to the office, and immediately to guards appeared beside Frank.

Frank deliberately did not look at the Wolf as he left. He kept his eyes down and in front of him. He was lost in his thoughts so much, that he found himself back at the bunkhouse without realizing that he had made the journey back across the frozen muck–filled yard.

That night, the nightmares began again.

It was March 27, twenty days of living in the Kingdom of Lice.

Frank hadn't gotten much sleep since his visit with The Wolf. The nightmares continued to worsen. Fear of being called in for 'questioning', combined with the lack of food and warmth, made him more desolate than ever. On the morning of March 27, he was leaning in the doorway of the bunkhouse, watching some of the guys play Blackjack. They used their dwindling supply of cigarettes as money. It wasn't too terribly interesting to watch, but it was a small distraction at least.

Pop...pop...

Frank stood up straight, not believing what he just heard. He leaned toward the door.

Pop...pop...pop...

That's gunfire! he realized and tore open the door to the bunkhouse.

A bullet punctured the wall to his left, only two feet away.

Frank flinched, but remained where he was.

Before him, he saw the gates to Stalag 13B had been blown wide open. Pouring through those gates were vehicles mounted with machine guns manned by American soldiers.

"What the hell's goin' on out there?" Frank heard someone behind him ask.

There was only one explanation.

Frank turned back to those behind him, "Grab what you can! We're being rescued!"

Chapter 17
Those Crazy Cowboy Americans

About 90 miles west of Hammelburg were General George Patton's headquarters, located near Aschafensberg Germany, just south of Frankfurt. On March 22, units of his Fifth Infantry Division had crossed the Rhine River, the first American outfit to do so. By noon, the entire Division was across, and the construction of pontoon bridges was well underway.

General Patton sat in the early morning bustle of his headquarters, drinking coffee. He dialed through to his CO, General Omar Bradley, as he was finishing his second cup of coffee and said, "Don't tell anyone but I'm across."

He couldn't suppress a smile that came to his face as he heard Bradley sputter over the phone.

"You mean the Rhine?"

"Absolutely, I sneaked a Division over last night."

"I'll be damned," said Bradley, "You're impressing the Hell out of me!"

"You bet your ass!" replied Patton.

He saw that the opportunity to drive forward deep into the heart of Germany was there. General Patton and British General Bernard Montgomery found themselves in a friendly rivalry of sorts, one General always trying to outdo the other. The original plan had been for Montgomery to get there first with a force of about 100,000 men on March 23. So when Patton got one up on the Brit, he felt very pleased with himself.

General William Hoge, a Brigadier General, received a curious order the next day from General Patton. It came by way of Major General Manton Eddy, of the 12th Corps.

"He wants me to do what?" Hoge replied.

Eddy kept a straight face. "General Patton wants you to create a Task Force to penetrate the German lines, travel 50 miles into their territory to Hammelburg, and liberate the POW camp there."

"What the hell is he thinking!" yelled Hoge, "I've had my division finish thirty–six hours of combat just taking the Aschaffenburg bridge! Not only that, I've got orders to move the Division north with the Third Army! This is too damn much! I'm burning my men up! That order is impossible! I won't do it! You understand me?"

Eddy nodded his head and left.

A couple of hours later, an aide handed Hoge the phone, "It's General Patton, sir."

Hoge took the receiver and put it to his ear.

"Bill," Patton's voice, which Hoge found irritatingly arrogant, "I understand you are resisting me on this. Don't do that."

"Sir," replied Hoge, "We're going to be pushing in on the 7th Army's Zone. This could be a real mess."

"You let me worry about that!" reassured Patton, "I've already cleared this with Bradley, so it's going to happen! Do I make myself clear?"

"But, sir..."

Patton's tone changed, something that Hoge didn't expect. "Bill, look, I know you're afraid of losing men and vehicles. I promise you, I'll replace every single man and vehicle you lose! I promise!"

Deep inside, Hoge cursed himself, knowing that he was the new kid on the block when it came to Division Commanders. His promotion was both a blessing and a curse, because it placed him at the low end of the seniority pole. He realized that he just did not have the clout or the balls to win this fight.

"Yes, sir. I'll get someone on it right away."

"Who?" asked Patton.

"Lieutenant Colonel Abrams, Sir."

"Good enough, I'll be by later today to check in with him."

"Yes, sir."

As Hoge hung up, there was one thought in his mind, "What's so important about Hammelburg?"

About this time, Major Al Stiller showed up at Hoge's headquarters, and heard Hoge's side of the conversation. Hoge turned to him, "He wants Hammelburg! Why in the hell would he want that place?"

Stiller, a member of Patton's staff, replied calmly, "His son–in–law, sir. Lieutenant Colonel John Waters is a POW there. That is the true purpose of the raid."

Hoge stared at Stiller in pure amazement.

Patton showed up at Abram's Command Post at 1000 hours. With his aid, Major Stiller, in attendance, along with General Hoge, he addressed the senior staff, "Who's gonna lead this Task Force?"

"I will, sir." Abrams replied, "I'm going to take Combat Command B."

"You will not!" barked Patton, "I want a small force and I don't want you leading it! I need you doing what you're doing now. Get me someone down the chain. So who is it gonna be?"

Patton poured the gasoline on the fire, knowing that he needed to make sure that this thing was a success. He adjusted his stance and tones, letting the men in his presence know that this was going to happen and it was going to happen properly.

The Lieutenant Colonel looked at the other officers for just a moment, before he returned his attention to Patton, "It's going to be Hal Cohen of the 10th Armored Infantry. That is...if his ass will let him."

"His ass?" smirked Patton, knowing full well what that meant, "You mean the man's got hemorrhoids? Oh hell, no! I'm not going to let some bleeding ass crash this mission! If Napoleon hadn't had this particular problem, he would've won Waterloo! Hell, no! Get someone in here right now! Let's look at this man's ass! If it's a bad ass, I don't want him going!"

Accompanied by a battalion surgeon, Patton and the rest of the officers in tow, visited Cohen's Headquarters. Inside, after the salutes were made, Patton took Cohen to the side for a brief conversation.

"I understand, son, that you have some physical restrictions right now. I hear you have a bad ass."

Cohen nodded, "Yes, sir. It's very sore, sir."

General Patton gestured toward an adjoining room, "Step in here and let the Doc and I have a look."

Cohen complied when he stepped into the room and obeyed the order to drop his pants and grab his ankles. Patton bent over and looked. What he saw appeared to be a half–a–dozen fleshy eggs hanging out of the man's ass. The doctor whistled in amazement.

"That's it then," said Patton, "Pull em up and button it! You're not going!"

The General returned to the other room where the other officers were waiting, "He's not going. Who else can go?"

"I think that Baum would do you well, sir," suggested Cohen.

"Who?" Patton asked.

Cohen gestured to a young officer standing away from the circle of commanders. Patton immediately strode over to Captain Abe Baum and pulled him to the side.

"Listen, Abe, I know you have an excellent combat record. You pull this off and I'll make sure that you get rewarded. Congressional Medal of Honor."

"Sir," Baum replied calmly, "I don't need to be bribed. If you order it, it'll happen, sir."

Patton nodded, satisfied with the man's answer. He turned back to Hoge, "We're done here." As Hoge followed the General out the door, Patton turned to Baum and said, "Major Stiller will fill you in."

Baum nodded in understanding.

Patton looked at the Command Staff before him, thinking to himself, *these men are fine officers. They'll get the job done.* He nodded to the group of officers and then turned around and vanished through the door.

Baum turned to Stiller, "What's so special about Hammelburg?"

Stiller returned the questioning look with a simplistic answer, "There are, according to our intelligence, 300 POWs there. He wants them liberated."

Stiller ignored Baum's skeptical expression. The officers knew that he knew the whole story, but he wasn't budging.

It was 2:30 a.m. when Baum, with a column of fifty–odd armored vehicles and tanks finally penetrated the German front and dove deep into the black German night. Baum cursed to himself. A battle that Intelligence had told them would only last no more than thirty minutes, lasted over five hours.

According to the report from the men, as soon as the first Sherman tank came within range of the town's cobbled street, a lone German with a *Panzerfaust* stopped the Sherman dead in its tracks, thus successfully blocking the way for the rest of the column to move forward and through the town.

Then the fight got nasty.

The Germans poured out of every foxhole, every village house, every alley there was, resisting the oncoming Americans, making them pay for every step in blood and metal. Finally, one man was able to reach the disabled Sherman tank, crank up the engine, and maneuver it to the side, clearing the way for the column to continue through Schweinheim.

Next came the "house cleaning."

The Infantry troops had the deadly job of going house–to–house, killing any German soldiers they found so the Task Force could advance unimpeded. The entire venture could have gone south at any moment, and several times, it almost did. But the Doughboys were persistent and tenacious.

If not for their bravery and ingenuity, Baum thought to himself, *this operation would have been dead before it started.*

As he rode in his peep (an amphibious jeep), Baum looked at Stiller, who was riding in the car behind him. Stiller was the odd man out on this mission.

An observer for the Third Army.

A Major to boot.

Baum didn't buy it.

Stiller wasn't telling him the whole story, and it ate at him.

After passing through Schweinheim, they sailed through five villages with very little resistance, but when they reached the town of Lohr, they came upon a barricade. As the lead Sherman started to clear it, a *Panzerfaust* took out the tank. Down one tank, the Task Force pressed onward.

Some time later, Baum's Task Force came upon a convoy of twelve camouflaged trucks, and after unleashing their 37mm cannons, left the convoy in smoking ruins. The next target was a rail town of Gemunden.

As they moved into the town, and the sun was starting to rise, the tanks destroyed a dozen trains. They moved cautiously into the town, which was known as a place of convergence for three rivers, the Main, the Sinn, and the Saale. Gemunden, meant "mouthing." Since this town was larger than the others they had encountered, Baum ordered strict radio silence and sent Lieutenant Nutto, who was in charge of the heavy tanks, ahead to quickly secure the bridge over the river Saale. Thus, the way would be opened for a direct route to Hammelburg.

Lieutenant Sutton went with Nutto. He was to direct the infantry's efforts to clear the houses surrounding the bridge over the Saale. As Nutto's lead tank moved forward, the tank driver saw an opportunity and took it. He fired upon a train that was slowly coming out of the station on a parallel track with the road. The first shell stopped the train like a giant invisible fist. The second and third shells ignited the ammunition cars behind it, creating a tremendous explosion.

Suddenly, all hell broke loose.

Machine guns and *Panzerfausts* were everywhere. Rockets and bullets filled the air like a giant swarm of bees.

The battle had begun.

At one point, Baum interrogated one of the enemy they had captured, only to learn that Gemunden was a marshalling area for two German divisions, and one of those divisions had unloaded from the night before! He stared at Major Stiller, who could not suppress his shock and surprise.

How in the hell, thought Baum, *are three hundred men going to fight an entire German division?*

Baum learned later that Lieutenant Sutton saw an opportunity for his infantry to make it across the bridge and ordered them to go. With two of his men halfway across, Sutton was certain they were going to make it. Nothing could stop his Doughboys.

The next moment, there was a metal shriek and simultaneous groan as the entire bridge lurched. Sutton's two infantrymen were gone, as was half the bridge.

Nutto realizing what had happened, quickly retreated back to Baum, "Sir! Bridge is blown! We can't stay here! They're killing us!"

Baum opened his mouth to reply, when there was a sharp dry *crack! Boom!*

As Baum opened his eyes, he found himself lying on the ground. His right hand was numb, and one of his knees was exposed to the bone. Covered in his own blood, he looked over and saw Nutto's leg torn open by the shell fragments that had injured him as well.

"Nutto, you can't stay here..." he said through the pain of his own wounds as the numbness wore off and the agony began to set in, "You're too hurt, head back to the half–track and lie down."

Nutto's face was a mixture of pain and anger and resistance to being sidelined. But he simply nodded his head as two Doughboys helped him to the back of the column.

Baum realized that he had to find another route to Hammelburg.

Quickly, Baum had his wounds bandaged by the medics and began studying the maps. There was a road to Burg Sinn with a road to Hammelburg. It was a longer route, but it was an alternative. The problem was in finding out if there was a bridge across the Jinn River in Burg Sinn.

Grabbing a German prisoner, he asked, "Is there a bridge across the Sinn at Burg Sinn?"

The German denied it, but after Baum got persuasive, he admitted that a bridge did exist there.

Baum gave the order: "Disengage! Disengage!"

Baum immediately directed them toward Burg Sinn. He kept the German prisoner with him in his jeep, to ensure his truthfulness. Leaving behind three smashed Sherman tanks and an unknown number of dead soldiers, Baum pressed forward.

Baum radioed the 4th Armored HQ, "Marshalling yards at Gemunden requires air strike."

After that message, HQ lost the Task Force. No one, including General Patton, knew where they were.

Task Force Baum arrived in Burg Sinn and ran into a German Staff car. Out of the car stepped four Germans, one of who wore a long leather coat adorned with golden epaulettes. He was a general, and Baum's prisoner.

Suddenly, Baum heard a very ominous sound.

An airplane.

The spotter plane circled overhead, and the Task Force unleashed everything they had, but it wasn't enough. Baum knew with certainty that the Germans now knew the size of his Task Force and their location.

According to a road sign, Hammelburg was nineteen kilometers away. Picking up a German civilian, they were guided to Grafendore. At Grafendore, the Task Force liberated several hundred Russian prisoners. It was March 27th.

They were closing on Hammelburg. Baum's Task Force had accessed a highway that would lead them to the camp. He didn't like the lay of the land. They were surrounded on all sides by high ground and Hammelburg lay ahead.

It wasn't until the first shell that missed, that Baum knew they were in a world of pain. Suddenly, from all sides the enemy opened fire. Baum would later learn that he was walking into a trap that was laid by a Haptmann Koehl, possessing numerous TDs (tank destroyers) known as *Ferdinands*.

Baum surveyed the situation and ordered the mounted 105's up to a knoll to return fire. "Sergeant Graham! Get up that knoll and kill those bastards!"

"Yes, sir!" was Graham's reply.

As Graham's 105's assaulted the Germans, Baum ordered his light tanks and half–tracks to slip through toward the camp. Baum and Stiller watched with fascination as the Shermans took on the heavier–plated German TDs. One–by–one, the Shermans were slowly dying.

His men, dying.

Task Force Baum lost five half–tracks, two jeeps, and sustained damage to most of the Shermans. Finally, Baum had had enough. He broke off the fight and pressed forward toward Stalag 13B.

The tanks reached the barbed wire in the Serbian section of the camp. The guards abandoned their posts, and the Americans rushed the section, greeting the tankers with shouts of joy.

Colonel Goode was elated at the prospect of being rescued, but he was concerned about the unintentional friendly fire that could injure the camp prisoners. He asked Lieutenant Colonel Waters to go out with him and a German liaison officer, a Captain Fuchs, and meet the tankers under a flag of truce.

John Waters walked calmly out of the bunkhouse toward the awaiting tankers. He held up a makeshift white flag. He could barely contain his excitement, as he and the rest of the men here in this Hellhole were about to be rescued. Beside him were Colonel Goode and Captain Fuchs.

Now if they don't kill any of our guys with friendly fire, then this thing's gonna be smooth all the way, he thought.

Just then, he saw a figure loom in the darkness ahead, just beyond a wooden fence. The man was camouflaged and aimed his rifle at them.

Instinctively, Waters said, *"Amerikanisch?"*

As the German liaison officer began to speak, the dark figure cursed and fired.

Waters fell to the ground, his entire body screaming in pain. It felt like his entire spine and everything connected to it was just infused with white–hot liquid steel.

Commandant Goekel had guards with rifles try to stop the tanks, but Baum swept over them and stopped at the barb–wire. The area where they entered was the Serbian part of the camp. The Serbian camp and American camp was separated by a wire gate. When the Kriegies saw the tanks, they rushed the gate and poured into the Serbian camp.

While Baum watched the Kriegies celebrate their immanent freedom, several questions plagued him.

First, "What the hell am I going to do with all these men?"

Second, "What about those who can't make the march back?" There were quite a number of starved faced and skinny bodies before him.

Third, and this was the most crucial, "Where was the way back?"

At Divisional Headquarters, on the morning of March 28, 1945, a single message came through at 0300.

MISSION ACCOMPLISHED

Chapter 17
Escape from Stalag 13B

"Hold on! Hold on!" shouted Jay, as they all scrambled at their bunks, gathering whatever they thought they would need and stuffing it into emptied pillowcases and makeshift backpacks that survived the Hellmarch.

Movement in the bunkhouse stopped as every man turned to look at Jay.

"Look," he explained, "We can't just run out there without knowing what is exactly happening out there! Gather your stuff...but for Pete's sake...wait until we know something!"

It made sense to Frank. He looked out the window. The tanks that had burst through the gates were moving aside to allow more US vehicles to pour into the campgrounds. There was a slowing of the firefight outside, from the sounds of gunfire.

"Hey! Look at that!" someone exclaimed, "Isn't that Colonel Waters?"

Frank and the other men rushed to the window.

Sure enough, it *was* Colonel Waters with the SAO Colonel Goode and a German officer, waving a makeshift white flag at the attacking soldiers. After a moment, they saw him, and ceased their gunfire.

"I bet he's trying to keep us from getting killed!" another man said.

"That would make sense," replied Dallas.

Frank watched as Colonel Waters, whom it was known that he was General Patton's son–in–law, walked toward the tanks, waving his white flag. Everyone knew he was General Patton's son–in–law. There was a moment of silence punctuated only by the purring of the massive tank engines. Colonel Waters was about halfway across the yard, when a single shot rang out.

Everyone stopped breathing.

Colonel Waters went down in a heap.

"Is he dead?" someone dared to ask.

A half–breath later, Waters moved his body, and Frank heard his cries of pain through the thin, frost–covered window pane.

Everyone, Frank included, sat in silence, hearts pounding...waiting for whatever was to happen next.

Five minutes passed like that...everyone holding their breath.

Then, a half–track pulled up from the invading column, and a man appeared with a bullhorn, "Attention US officers and other prisoners of Stalag 13! We are from the Fourth Armored Division, sent here to rescue you! Let every able–bodied man come forward and let's get you the hell out of here!"

A roar of joy escaped from every man in that bunkhouse, and Frank joined them.

He was going home!

Approximately an hour later, at six o'clock, the armored column of sixty–plus vehicles began their escape from Stalag 13B. Frank was sitting on the hood of a half–track, hanging on to a handrail, while the night began to settle around them. He knew that they had to move fast because night around here became black as pitch.

It had taken about forty–five minutes to round up as many men as the armored vehicles could carry, in addition to those men who decided to walk with the column out of the camp. Camp SAO, Colonel Goode, had met with the Captain who had led the assault, a Captain Abraham Baum. Both of them were at the head of the column. Frank learned that this raiding party consisted of about two–hundred and sixty–six men, and sixty–plus armored vehicles. It was enough of a force to apparently punch through the German lines and travel deep into enemy territory to Hammelburg. The driver of the half–track, Adams, was telling them as much as he could while he kept his eyes on the vehicle in front of him.

It was hard to do.

Frank had learned during the Hellmarch that German nights were infamous for their utter blackness. He tried to listen to Adam's voice while he gripped the handrail on the half–track as hard as he could.

"Yeah!" Adams was laughing, "You shoulda seen them Krauts' faces when we punched through that line and kept on going! I don't know German, but I do know what the universal facial expression, 'What the hell?' looks like! Hoo boy! That's a sight I'll never forget!"

"What about Colonel Waters?" someone shouted at Adams.

"Waters? I think that Kraut shot him in the spine! Nasty bastard! Got what he had coming to him for doing that to a man wavin' a white flag! I think we had to leave him behind! Too messed up to carry with us!"

"That was some bravery. Him and Colonel Goode, I mean, for walking out there like that," said Dallas, nearly yelling it over the sound of the engine.

"I'd say so!" agreed Adams.

The column of vehicles plowed through the pitch black night, lights off so they couldn't be tracked. How Adams was able to see the vehicle in front of him was beyond Frank, but he was grateful for the man's skill.

Ten minutes later, disaster struck.

The engine died.

"What the hell?" Adams cursed. He tried turning it over several times, but the half–track stubbornly sat there, while other vehicles in the column passed them by.

Frank felt his hopes start to sink.

I can't go back. We're so close! So close!

"What's wrong?" someone asked.

"I sure as hell wish I knew!" barked Adams. Frank got off the hood so Adams could raise it and look at the engine.

"Aw...for Pete's sake!" Adams cried out.

"How bad is it?" asked Jay.

"The only way we're movin' this baby is if we push!" declared the driver.

Just then, another vehicle pulled up alongside, and the driver leaned out his window: "Hey! Need a lift?"

He was driving, for lack of a better term, a military–sized 8–ton tow–truck.

Frank's spirits began to lift again.

Maybe there is a God.

After joining the column again, being pulled behind the towing vehicle, Frank was certain that they were only hours from freedom.

He could taste it.

Smell it.

Feel it.

At the rate of speed they were going, Frank knew that if they hit a bad patch in the road and he lost his grip, even for a moment, he could find himself under the wheels and treads within a heartbeat. Then it would be bye–bye Frank.

Almost an hour passed before they slowed to stop. The reason, it turned out, was that the US forces had captured a German PX truck and put it on the side of the road. Other vehicles had stopped and the men were getting off and raiding the truck. Frank decided that this was a good idea.

He hopped off the half–track and made his way to the PX truck. After grabbing two loaves of bread, he clambered back onto his spot. Once other men on their vehicle had grabbed what they could, they started up again, and proceeded down the column.

This bid for freedom wasn't easy, as Frank learned.

After about twenty minutes, the driver of the 8–ton wrecker stopped, and got out. Frank saw that other vehicles were turning around. The driver walked back to them and explained what was happening.

"German *Panzerfaust*. They've taken out three of our tanks."

"Dammit!" Adams swore.

"Everyone is turning around while we can to another route we discovered. Just keep on praying you guys."

"You betcha!" Adams said.

Frank found himself praying.

They were short prayers.

But he was praying.

By Adams's estimation, they had traveled about ten miles from Stalag 13B when they stopped. The remaining attack vehicles had made a perimeter in a large field, surrounding the smaller transport vehicles. Every man was asked to report to the center where Captain Baum and Colonel Goode had called for an assembly.

Frank joined the other men, and they waited until all the remaining vehicles had been accounted for.

Colonel Goode addressed them in a somber tone.

"Men, I'm going to cut to the chase. When Captain Baum broke through the German front lines, they didn't know what to think. As a result, we can only conjecture that they presumed this to be a reconnaissance in force. As such, we have reports that they are sending two Divisions of enemy troops to capture us."

Silence reigned.

Frank was stunned.

Two Divisions! God in heaven! They were dead!

"The Germans, by now, realize that this was a rescue action. As such, they will be all out to recapture every man who escaped from Stalag 13B. I have spoken to the Fourth Armored Division who spearheaded this mission. They have advised us that we are on our own. I repeat...they cannot reach us in time. According to the last report I received, the German forces will be here within an hour. Therefore, I present to you one of two options. Grab a rifle and prepare for a hell of firefight. Or you can return with me to Stalag 13B under our own power. We begin our march in ten minutes. Decide now. That is all."

There was an immediate chorus of voices as men began to discuss what they wanted to do.

Frank looked down at the ground, thinking.

They always said to me, "If you get out of the camp, you've got a 50/50 shot of freedom. Take it!" But if I stay here, I'm gonna get chewed up in a bloody mess, that's for sure. I can't go back to that camp. I can't. I won't. Of course, there is a third option.

Jay Drake was standing next to Frank, lost in his own thoughts as well.

"Jay?" said Frank quietly, "You thinking what I'm thinking?"

Jay's eyes met his in the light of the vehicle's headlamps, "That we just hit the hills and keep on running? I've got this tiny compass that the Red Cross smuggled in." He held up a tiny, thumb–nail sized compass. There was a look in his eyes that Frank knew mirrored the one in his own.

"How much ground could we cover in a day?" Frank asked, still keeping his voice low.

"Forget about daytime, Frank," answered Jay, "We've got to move at night. It's safer."

"Yeah, you're right."

I've got this bread. That should last us a little while. We need some water. And a knife or two.

Frank looked around until he found Dallas.

"Dallas, I need your canteen," he said hastily.

Dallas was as straight–faced as Frank had ever seen him when he answered, "No, Frank, I can't do that."

Frank started to panic, "What? Why not?"

Dallas tilted his head to the side, with a gleam in his eye that matched Jay's, "Cause I'm going with you."

Frank's panic turned into a surge of hope.

"Fine...let's go."

The three men, carrying nothing but their wits, two loaves of bread, and a water canteen, walked out of the perimeter of tanks and armored vehicles and into the edge of the trees that surrounded the field.

Half–an–hour later, the shelling began.

Chapter 18
Thank God for Fog and Hunters!

The screaming crash of shells spurred Frank, Dallas, and Jay on. Behind them were the sounds of a ferocious battle. It more than justified Frank's decision.

There was another reason why Frank picked Jay to join him.

Jay grew up in Michigan and was a deer hunter at an early age. The woods were his natural environment. He knew things about surviving in the wild that Frank never even suspected. In his mind, Frank had nominated Jay as their de–facto leader. He made a mental note to give Jay the lead in their decisions.

Behind and all around them, were the sounds of men crashing through the woods, other GIs, Frank was certain, who had the same idea as he did. At the same time, he reminded himself that two Divisions were converging on the area, and their only hope was to lay low at every possible moment.

The three of them crept through the woods, trying their best to not make any sound, but their footfalls were amplified by the crunch of the dead leaves underfoot. Frank cursed to himself silently, but there was nothing else they could do, they had to keep moving.

After about twenty minutes, they heard the distinct and frightening sound of a machine gun over the next rise. Jay pantomimed a clumsy sign for creeping slowly, and Frank and Dallas nodded their heads in understanding. The three of them knelt down as low as they could and slowly crept up to the tip of the rise.

Two hundred yards in front of them sat a machine gun nest at the edge of a field. The gunners were firing at any movement they detected. Many times after they fired, the movement they heard or saw...stopped. The brilliant staccato flashes of the muzzle was at once terrifying and sobering. One wrong move or sound...

Jay touched his shoulder and motioned for them to retreat back down the rise. Frank followed...slowly.

At the bottom of the rise, they discussed their options.

"There's no way we can get across that field," said Jay.

"We'll get cut to pieces," said Dallas.

Frank looked around, his eyes desperately seeking another way. Then he saw a large pine tree with heavy hanging boughs. He had an idea.

"Okay, what if we wait until this excitement passes? What if we lay low in one spot until that nest moves? They surely can't stay there forever? Right?"

"What do you have in mind, Frank?" asked Jay.

Frank pointed to the pine tree, which was about twenty feet away. "See that pine tree? We clear out the leaves around it, stack them up to hide ourselves, and when it's safe, then we move. It's just too dangerous right now to be out there when we don't know friend from foe."

"I agree," said Dallas.

"Okay," answered Jay, "Let's do this."

The three of them crept over to the pine tree, scooped out the leaves and needles and heaped them up around the tree, so no one would see anything unusual unless they walked directly upon that particular tree.

Then they waited, listening to gunfire echoing through the cold night air.

Day One

Knowing that they couldn't move during the day, they stayed there, under the pine tree until dark.

Frank's instincts were telling him to get up and run as far as they could, but rational thought prevailed. *No...if I have to stay under this pine tree until an American finds us...so be it.*

At dark, about eight o'clock, the three of them began to move again. They walked for about two hours through the woods, and finally came out half–a–mile or so from where the machine gun nest was positioned. The clearing before them was lit up by the brilliant moon that shone down from above.

"Jay," said Frank, "if we walk out there, they'll see us."

"I know," he replied.

It was ten o'clock.

They sat there at the edge of the clearing, waiting for something to happen.

It did.

They fell asleep.

Day Two

Frank awoke with a start.

It was still night–time.

In fact, glancing at his watch, it was midnight.

He looked at Jay and Dallas, also asleep.

Frank's face was damp, he realized, and then he noticed his surroundings. A thick fog, as thick as pea soup, blanketed the entire area. Frank couldn't see five feet ahead of him.

He shook Jay and Dallas awake gently.

"What...?" said Dallas sleepily.

"A fog, you guys! We got ourselves a fog!" Frank tried hard to keep his voice down but strained against his excitement.

Jay's eyes opened wide when he realized what this meant, "We can..."

"...cross over!" finished Dallas.

They rose as quickly as they could and began to cross the fog–covered clearing.

Five miles later, they found a thicket of trees they could hide in. Tired from the walking and excitement, they made themselves as comfortable as possible and fell asleep. Exhaustion and the prospect of freedom was a heavy narcotic, and they all remained unconscious until morning.

As Frank woke up and came to his senses, he began to listen to the various sounds around them. He could tell that there was a road, a river, and a bridge nearby.

Using the bread that he had acquired from the PX truck, and some rations that Dallas and Jay had gained from the men in the rescue unit, they ate a satisfying meal that morning. Seeing how it was now day-light, there was no way they could move freely.

The road and bridge nearby, perhaps two hundred—or—so yards, were cramped with activity. They decided that if they went walking down the road, they would run into soldiers. If they tried to cross the bridge, they would run into soldiers. If they waited until nightfall, things might be different.

So they spent a day in that thicket of trees, resting and gathering their strength.

No one said anything frivolous. This wasn't a time for a political discussion or reminiscing about your girlfriend.

So they waited.

Eventually, night came.

With Jay leading them, they began moving toward the direction of the river. About fifty yards from the road, Jay held up a hand, signaling them to stop. He cupped his hand to his ear. *Listen.*

Sure enough, Frank heard the voices and footsteps of a regiment of German soldiers marching down the road. The three of them remained where they were, waiting for the soldiers to pass.

Frank found himself holding his breath much of the time, afraid to even breathe loudly.

Eventually, the German soldiers passed, and the three men slipped out of the woods, across the road, and down to the riverbank. Fashioning a small raft using their Polish overcoats and two small logs, they began to cross the river. Dallas jumped into the river first carrying the raft with their provisions across. Frank and Jay followed.

They had stripped down to their bare skin, and Frank had never experienced a cold like this before. Halfway across the twenty—five yards of river, his teeth began to chatter.

This is colder than blazes!

Swimming was never his strong suit, and he was holding his clothes high above him. But somehow they all got across, and dressed again. Frank shared some of his dry clothes with them because they had gotten their clothes wet.

Once on the other side of the river, they found themselves faced with a cliff. Slowly and with much effort, they began to climb.

"Can we take a break?" Dallas asked.

"I think that's a good idea," answered Frank.

"What kind of food do we have left?" asked Jay.

Upon examination, they found that they still had some of the bread that Frank had stolen from the PX truck along with a tin of uncooked bacon. Dallas broke the bread into chunks and Jay laid the raw bacon on it.

Their stomachs grumbled horribly until the food hit their bellies.

Despite the dark, (the moon was hiding this night), Frank could tell that the other two men were enjoying the meal, as was he.

"Tastes as good as cake!" declared Frank.

"Hear hear!" answered Jay.

"I'll second that!" replied Dallas.

Day Three

The rain began to fall soon after they conquered the cliff.

They quickly decided that they needed shelter.

As they moved through the woods, they began to find small farms and houses, signs of a small mountain village. However, they could tell that the houses were occupied.

They obviously couldn't break into someone's house while they were there...that would only result in their recapture. So they continued to move from house to house, searching for shelter from the rain.

A good thing these villagers don't have guard dogs, Frank thought to himself.

At least, they hadn't happened upon one yet.

Finally, they found a house that looked abandoned, but it was all boarded up and impossible to get into without making a tremendous amount of noise. Frank's hopes began to sink until Jay's whispers beckoned them to join him behind the house.

It was there they found a small storage garage, with a tiny loft and a ladder leaning on the outside which they could use to get inside through the small window at the top of the garage.

I guess I have you to thank for this... Frank glanced upward to sky above.

Closing the door tight, Frank, Jay, and Dallas got themselves as comfortable as possible. When Frank looked at his watch one last time, it read five–thirty.

At nine–thirty, Frank awoke to distant sounds of shouting. He reached out with a hand and gently shook Dallas and Jay awake. Both came to with a start.

They peered out the eaves of the garage, and saw before them a beautiful mountain valley. A road and river ran down the center and branched off in two directions. A bridge rested right at the neck of the branch.

At first sight, Frank thought that the bridge would be a great place to cross. Then he saw a squad of Germans move toward the bridge, carrying explosives with them.

They're mining the bridge! There goes that plan!

"Look over there!" Dallas pointed.

Frank looked and saw a squad of Germans, burp guns out, surrounding what looked like a small group of about twenty soldiers.

"They look like Russians..." Jay said.

"Yeah," said Frank, feeling helpless and frustrated at the same time. He couldn't help his mixed feelings of guilt and gratitude that they hadn't been caught, "Captain Baum said they freed about a thousand Russians. Those poor guys."

The German guards were not being friendly or hospitable either. Several Russians looked bruised and beaten.

"Uh guys," Jay pointed, "We better get out of here!"

When Frank looked at where he pointed, he saw a lone German walking toward the abandoned house that was positioned in front of the garage.

Sticking point first into the wooden post of the doorframe to the garage, was a farmer's work knife, with barely a layer of dust on it. Looking back at the approaching German, Frank moved next to the door ever so quietly.

As Frank reached out toward the knife and realized with horror something was terribly wrong.

His hands were ungloved.

What happened to my gloves?

He tried to remember what he did with them.

Where? Where? Where?

He spun around, knife in hand, looking for where they could have fallen. Where were those damned gloves?

Then the memory came to him, like a splash of cold water.

In helping with the ladder, he took them off.

Frank glanced through the cracks in the doorway.

He had taken them off.

Outside.

They lay right outside —where they could be seen by anyone.

He glanced back up, trying to locate the German.

There was a knothole that was positioned just so he could look out it and see the approaching man. From this vantage point, Frank could see the man's face clearly.

His blood turned to ice, and he gripped the knife in his hand as tightly as he could.

It was The Wolf.

Chapter 19
My God Saves Me!

Frank held his breath.

The Wolf turned his back to him. He was only five or six yards from the door to the garage. Frank risked a glance back at Jay and Dallas.

They were frozen in place, but their eyes spoke volumes.

*Do what you need to do...*said Jay's.

I trust you! said Dallas's.

Frank nodded his head and placed a shushing finger to his lips.

They both nodded in assent.

Frank turned back to the knothole and peered out.

The Wolf was turning back toward the garage. His eyes looked up at the sky, then the top of the building. As they dropped down, Frank felt his body tense.

When The Wolf saw Frank's gloves, his eyes widened.

He looked around, and then stepped...ever so slowly...toward them, as though they were a bear–trap. He tossed his cigarette away and bent down, with one gloved hand reaching for the gloves. Standing up, he peered at them, examining them closely.

Then he brought his gaze upon the garage door.

Without any further hesitation, Frank threw open the door, knife in one hand, the other hand reaching for the Wolf's coat. Before the German could cry out or anything, he was pulled into the garage.

Frank placed the point of the blade directly on the Wolf's neck.

The Wolf's eyes were wide with...surprise? Fear? Frank couldn't tell, and he didn't really care either.

"Well...well...Herr Battle. Look at where we have met!"

"Shut up!" hissed Frank.

The Wolf smiled...a knowing smile...a predatory smile...a smile of a man who knows he's won the game..."Imagine the fortuitous set of circumstances that have led you and I to this moment right here!"

"I said...*shut up!*" Frank was trying to contain his rage but was failing at it.

"Very well...I will...as you say...shut up...but you will not get very far in your objective if I do..."

"What is he talking about?" asked Jay.

"He's talking about us using him to get information on how to get out of this area..." replied Dallas, "Isn't he, Frank?"

The Wolf's eyes lingered on Jay and Dallas long enough to take in their faces, then his eyes focused back on Frank.

"You have very wise and perceptive allies, Herr Battle."

"I said..."

"I know...I know...shut up," replied the Wolf.

"Frank...we can use him..." said Dallas, "He can tell us where to go..."

"He can also lead us right into a trap..." said Jay.

The Wolf's eyes remained fixed on Frank.

"What to do...?" mused the Wolf.

Frank couldn't think. It was too hard to think right now. He was so...blind with rage. He had to calm down.

"Dallas..." he said.

"Yeah," was the reply.

"Get his gun..."

Dallas moved forward and reached into the Wolf's overcoat, withdrawing from it a side–arm. He checked the chamber.

"It's loaded."

"Good...Jay...take his coat..."

Jay moved, and stripped the Wolf of his overcoat.

"Search him, Dallas..."

Dallas handed the pistol to Jay, who kept it trained on the Wolf, while Dallas began to pat down the German. Frank continued to hold the knife at his throat. The Wolf offered no resistance.

"You think you hold my life in your hands...Herr Battle..."

"Shut up!"

The Wolf ignored him, "But it is I who continue to hold yours in mine...what should happen if I don't return to the troops soon? Hmmm? I'll tell you...they will begin searching...and they will find you!"

Dallas produced a pair of metal cuffs for prisoners from a belt attachment. "Look what I found!"

"Good!" said Frank, "Use them on him!"

At that moment, the Wolf moved without any hint or indication of attack...his face still the same cold, impassive, predatory expression. He brought his hands up, simultaneously hitting Frank under the chin and under his arms, while leaning his head back, out of the way of a potentially fatal cut. Frank lost his grip on the knife and it went spinning into the air overhead. The Wolf brought his right elbow smashing into Dallas's nose, and pushing him back into Jay, who couldn't get a clean shot on the German.

Suddenly, as Frank's eyes cleared, he saw a small dagger appear in the Wolf's right hand, where it came from, Frank had no idea. The Wolf lunged forward and Frank backed up, barely dodging a slash to his face. Suddenly, the Wolf turned on him and spun around to face Dallas, who was holding his face, blood gushing from his nose, and Jay, who was trying to recover his wits about him to use the gun.

Frank saw his knife land, point down in the wooden floor. Grabbing it, he rushed forward, embracing the Wolf from behind.

He felt the blade sink into the man's back.

The Wolf's face was one of shock and disbelief. He gasped for air, and bloody spittle appeared on his lips.

Frank hissed in his ear, "You want to know something, Herr Wolf? You asked me a question a while back...didn't you?" With that, Frank jerked the knife a fraction.

The Wolf's eyes were wide with pain, but also comprehension. He heard everything Frank was saying. The agony he felt crushed any ability he had to cry out. He gasped for air.

"What was it?...Oh yes...you asked me where my God is?...didn't you?" Frank jerked the blade a little more forcefully this time, and more blood began to appear on the Wolf's lips.

Jay and Dallas were no longer there.

The garage was no longer there.

The soldiers outside were no longer there.

It was just Frank and the Wolf.

Just Frank and the Wolf.

"You know what I figured out? Wolfie?..." Frank hissed, "That you aren't a God at all...Are you?" another jerk of the knife, and more blood, deep black, began to flow from the German's mouth.

Frank savored this moment.

"No...you aren't a God at all...You're a beast! A beast that needs to be put down!" A final sharp jerk of the knife, and it was suddenly free of the man's body. The Wolf fell to the ground, black blood pouring from his mouth, choking him, eyes wide with terror, fear, and every other emotion that Frank knew this monster had relished inflicting on others. The man's pain was so intense that as he lay there, his back arched, his lungs gasping for air through the knife wound that had pierced his right lung, severing it in two.

Frank leaned down and stared at the Wolf's eyes as the life started to drain from them. He whispered softly to the man.

"You asked where my God was? He's right here. He gave us shelter for the night and a knife to kill you with...You see...Wolfie...My God saves me...Yours just damns you...Enjoy your stay in hell...You bastard!"

The Wolf's eyes remained open, but the light that illuminated them faded.

And with that...the Wolf died.

And Frank Battle lived.

"Let's get out of here..." said Frank, not looking at the body of the Wolf.

Dallas leaned down and searched the man's body, finding a cloth to put on his nose to stop the bleeding, the small dagger that the Wolf had in his hand, and two clips of bullets that he gave to Jay.

"Ok..." Dallas said, his voice sounding funny from the broken nose, "I'm ready..."

With that, the three of them slipped out the back of the garage so they wouldn't be seen by the troops on the road. When they were about half—way to the woods, Frank stumbled across a box, lying in the middle of the field. It laid on its side, spilling its contents onto the snowy ground.

Frank couldn't believe it.

Candy.

It was candy...and lots of it.

Without further thought, Frank picked up the box of candy and resumed running for the cover of the trees.

They found a stand of fir trees where they rested for a few moments until Jay said, "We need to put some distance between us and that garage. As soon as they find him..." he left the rest unsaid, because it didn't need saying.

Frank nodded in agreement as he chewed on a chocolate bar.

Dallas said nothing. He just held the cloth to his nose, checking to see if the bleeding had stopped.

"Ten minutes..." Frank said between bites, "Give me ten minutes..."

"Sure," Jay replied, eyes scanning the area back from where they had come.

Ten minutes passed, and during that time, they decided to head north, following the path of one of the river tributaries. They kept moving, even when they recognized Allied planes flying overhead. A couple of times, they waved to them, trying to get their attention. Later that night, Frank wondered at why they didn't get strafed or bombed. They were in enemy territory, and there was no way to let their side know where or even who they were!

Eventually, they came to a spillway on the river, and found that someone Upstairs was continuing to look out for them.

Logs had been dragged from the river banks into the spillway in such a way that it made it possible to cross it by crawling on the logs. It took some time, but they did cross it without incident.

Moving into the woods beyond the water, Frank wondered what else lay ahead.

*Whatever is ahead...*he thought, *I can leave those nightmares behind now...*

Days Four, Five, and Six
The following days passed in a blur in Frank's mind.

They had reached virgin territory.

Following the guidance of Jay's compass and the sound of artillery fire indicating where the battle front was located, they moved through untouched woods. The forests around them stretched for miles in either direction, but they kept a tight course toward what they believed to be the Western Front.

Several times they heard small arms fire, pitched battles occurring a mile or two away, but they remained within the cover of the forests. They continued to move at night, when it was safest. During the day, they rested.

Dallas had also claimed the Wolf's lighter, but Frank and Jay both were too cautious about fire to allow him to use it to create a campfire. It seemed that these timber–filled lands would never end.

And so the days passed.

Then...on the seventh day, a shell landed nearby. It was four in the morning.

The three of them moved into a thicket and waited for the day to arrive.

After two to three hours of waiting, they heard the sound of engines and tanks.

What struck Frank was the sound of the vehicles.

It was just over the next hill, but far enough away that he couldn't tell if it was an American or German engine. The Germans used ersatz gas, which made their engines sound like, "hopa–chika–hopa–chika" whereas the American engines were a smooth purring sound.

Frank turned to Jay, "I want to go ahead and see what kind of vehicles those are..."

Jay shook his head, "I don't think it's safe, Frank. Best to stay put."

"But we need to know!" insisted Frank.

"Frank, I don't think you should risk it," said Dallas.

But something inside of him, call it desperation or curiosity, Frank wasn't sure which, forced itself to the fore, "I'm going," he declared.

With that, he moved out of the thicket and began crawling on the ground toward the noise. He had traveled about ten yards beyond the edge the clearing, in full sight of the road, when the vehicles came around the hill.

Frank, barely concealed, was terrified.

Leading this column of vehicles was a staff car carrying three or four senior German officers, three Germans riding motorbikes, a transport truck carrying a dozen–or–so German troops. The vehicles stopped twenty yards from Frank's position.

The officers exited the car, the rest of the vehicles stopping. They stood there, placing what looked like a map on the hood of the car, discussing something.

Frank was in agony.

He couldn't move.

He dared not to breathe.

Despite the cold, he felt a bead of sweat form on his forehead.

He couldn't even wipe away the sweat as it rolled down his head and into his eyes, stinging them with saltiness.

He remained completely still, trying not to breathe.

Five minutes passed...

The officers continued to talk.

Ten minutes passed...

Frank couldn't believe this...he had been sooo close to freedom...

Fifteen minutes passed...

If they catch me...what will I do?

Then...suddenly, it seemed...the German officers reached an agreement, folded up their maps, and entered the car again. They pulled forward, and passed Frank's position without a hint of knowing that he was there, almost in plain sight.

It wasn't until the final vehicle had passed and been gone five minutes before Frank stood up and ran back to where Jay and Dallas waited.

Please don' t let me be that stupid again! he chided himself.

Day Seven

That night it was black as pitch again.

They had been walking until they reached a place where the forest ran south, and they needed to continue to west. It was midnight, and they walked about five yards out from the edge of the forest.

"I think we need to follow the trees..." Dallas was saying.

"No..." argued Jay, "we need to head west, toward the Front..."

Suddenly, Frank heard something that was unbelievable to him, and quite frightening.

He heard a whispering sound...

"Shhh!" he hissed at both of them.

Dallas and Jay fell silent, a look of confusion in their faces.

Frank cupped his hand to his ear. Listen.

They fell silent.

They all heard it then...and it was whispering!

But the voices were speaking in German!

"Guys," said Frank very softly, "Let's just walk away...very slowly... they can't see us...we can't see them..."

The others nodded.

Following their training, they dropped low and began to creep away from the German whispering.

Once again, the darkness was their friend.

They continued on in the night, going in a perpendicular direction away from the whispering Germans until they found a road. They were only a mile down the road when out of nowhere, it seemed, a massive German appeared ahead of them.

To Frank he looked to be eight feet tall.

He was dressed in civilian clothes, carrying a gunnysack over his shoulder.

"Be cool..." Jay said quietly.

The civilian eyed them, cautiously, but as he passed he said, *"Morgen!"*

"Morgen!"

"Morgen!"

"Morgen!"

Frank kept his eyes forward and down.

It wasn't until a full two minutes had passed that he risked a glance backward to find that the civilian still walking his route.

Dallas let out a sigh of relief, "Wasn't expecting that!"

"Me neither," said Jay.

They found another thicket of trees off to the right–hand side of the road and bedded down for the night, thankful for their non–military appearances.

As the daylight broke over them that morning, Frank, Jay, and Dallas awoke to a company of about fifty troops marching down the road that they had just been on. The three of them sat in the thicket all day, watching troops pass by.

They also saw several civilians walk a small path through the woods, which, upon exploration, led to some crop fields a short distance away. Feeling trapped, Frank thought about the fact that they had almost resorted to living like animals. The hunted animal that doesn't move is the one that remains undiscovered, he surmised.

The three of them remained in the thicket all day...trapped like animals...unwilling to move.

When night fell, their spirits began to lift again.

Westward they continued.

Day Eight

Later that night, around two or three o'clock, they came upon a barn. Sneaking into the building, they snuck into the hay loft and situated themselves at the very back of the loft, covering themselves with the hay. The scent of the fresh hay was somewhat comforting, but what made things worst was that they had run out of food.

Frank's thoughts were on his stomach as he fell asleep.

He was awakened about six in the morning, by the sound of children jumping up and down in the hay mow. He watched as their father, carrying a pitchfork, was tossing hay down to the stock to feed the horses. Frank raised his head very slightly, but the father and the children didn't see him because he was concealed by the hay.

After a few minutes, the farmer and the children went back downstairs. Frank, Jay, and Dallas spent the whole day in the hay mow in the barn, but they could see down into the barnyard. The family dog kept walking up and down the barnyard, and Frank was certain that he could smell them, but the farmer and children never realized what the dog was growling at.

The kids kept telling the dog to, *"Shutupenze!"*

Frank, Jay, and Dallas agreed.

Shutupenze! Shutupenze! Shutupenze!

That night, about nine o'clock, they decided to leave the barn. As they landed on the first floor, they discovered a bin of potatoes.

They peeled the potatoes and devoured them hastily. Their grumbling stomachs were very grateful.

Cooked or uncooked.

Food was food.

To say they were in bad shape was an understatement, Frank realized as they walked.

Whereas days before they had been able to cover a mile in fifteen minutes, now they could only walk about two hundred and fifty yards in that same amount of time.

We're losing it here. How much longer can we keep pushing ourselves?

A moment later, something rebellious answered that thought.

As long as it takes!

Frank pushed on.

Westward.

Ever westward.

Day Nine

They had reached the end of the forest.

Below them stretched out a massive valley, which held no trees thick enough to hide in.

"We've got to turn around..." Dallas said.

"Let me do some looking around..." volunteered Jay.

"Fine, but just be careful," said Frank, too tired to move any further.

Jay moved off while Frank and Dallas stayed at the edge of the valley that stretched out below.

They sat there without talking. Talking took too much energy.

The sun began to rise.

It seemed like an hour passed before Jay returned.

"I found a more secure place..." he announced, "Follow me."

They did at a very slow pace.

Their exhaustion and hunger, was taking its toll on all of them.

It was an unseen specter that haunted them, day and night.

It took them longer to reach the place Jay had found than it had taken for Jay to find it and return to them. By that time, it was about ten o'clock.

They looked down, through the thicket, onto a road about a mile away. Proceeding up and down that road, were several U.S. Army vehicles.

Immediately, Jay and Frank exclaimed: "It looks like we made it! Those are American vehicles!"

Dallas, the pessimist, said, "No...those were captured in the Battle of the Bulge and the Germans are using them!"

Frank said, "It appears to me, that the road seems to bend toward our woods. Let's walk over there and try to get a little closer."

It wasn't too long before they heard the sound of a massive two–ton truck coming around the bend. As it passed, Frank, Jay, and Dallas, felt their spirits soar for the first time in many days.

Painted on the driver's side of the truck was a huge white Armed Forces Star.

Jay pointed to another vehicle coming around the bend, a Jeep, carrying two American soldiers.

"Do those look like Krauts to you, Dallas?"

Frank wasn't sure who was first out of the thicket, maybe it was all of them.

It didn't occur to him the sight they must have been, bolting out of the forest with ten–days growth of beards, long Polish overcoats hanging on skeletal frames, waving arms in the air. No...it didn't occur to him until the Jeep pulled over and both officers drew out their 45s and aimed them directly at them.

Oh my God! We made it and now we get shot!

One of the soldiers barked, "Who are you? Keep your hands raised!"

"No! No!" protested Jay.

"You don't understand!" shouted Dallas at the same time.

"We're Americans!" insisted Frank, "American officers! We escaped from Stalag 13!"

Then, all at once, Frank, Dallas, and Jay said in unison, "Don't shoot us!"

The American officers kept their guns trained on them.

Frank, Jay, and Dallas pulled out their dog tags, yelling, and "Dog tags Dog tags! We're escaped prisoners of war!"

With that, the officers lowered their weapons and said, "Where the hell have you been? We've been looking for you! There's an Engineers' headquarters about half–a–mile up the road. They're looking for you!"

So Frank, Jay, and Dallas walked down the road, and ten minutes later, they reached the headquarters and checked in. There they found some other escaped POWs. A Captain from the 28th Division advised them that now they were a part of the twenty–five POWs who had escaped from Stalag 13B and made it back to the American lines.

Shortly thereafter, the three "escapees" had a bath and threw their lice–infested clothes into a barrel, but the only clothes the engineers had for them were some tropical kakis uniforms. Frank thought they looked weird, but they were tolerable.

That night, when Frank, finally lay in a normal bunk bed, he could not get to sleep. All through his captivity, in camp, and on the road, he had never had a problem sleeping on the road. But the first night back in American–controlled territory, he suffered from a severe case of jangled nerves.

That was the only time it ever happened.

Chapter 20
Legacy
2010

Emmett Dumas leaned forward, intent on Frank's narration.

"We discovered, over the course of the days that followed, that we were only three of twenty–five men who actually successfully escaped from that larger number of seven–hundred men from Stalag 13B."

"And you arrived on what day?" the reporter asked.

"It was April 6, 1945, when we were discovered by Allied Forces. It took us nine days to cross about fifty miles of German territory. We were a mess. They had to burn our clothes because they smelled so bad. So for the first few days, we wore some tropical uniforms, we looked like...well...you know. They wanted us to go to the hospital, but we were too macho for that. Truth was, we should have gone to the hospital."

"How did you sleep?"

"For the first eight hours that I was back, my nerves were shot. You know the term jangling nerves? Well, I had a case of jangling nerves. Now I know what they are!"

"What happened next?"

"They sent us on the reverse supply route. Every time a delivery came in with supplies, we would ride back with them into Allied terri-tory. Every time someone, anyone, found out that we three were ex–POWs, they treated us like heroes. They gave us cigarettes, PX candy and rations, anything they felt like they could give. By the time we made it to Paris, France, we had a whole bunch of loot!"

"What was Paris like?"

"Nice. In fact, we were sitting in a Red Cross coffee and donut bar, talking about our experiences. We let it slip that we were ex–POWs and that if it weren't for the Red Cross, we wouldn't have made it. The next thing I know, there's a man asking the three of us to follow him to his boss, who was the Director for the Red Cross in Paris! So we went up to Director's office, where he and his staff asked us many questions about our POW experiences and how the Red Cross parcels were very essential to our well being. About eleven o'clock in the evening, we tried to excuse ourselves from the Director's office, and he said, 'No, no! You can't leave! Our chef is preparing you a five–course meal in the next room!' It was very extravagant...very nice of them to do that...very nice. By the time we got out of there, it was two o'clock in the morning and we had to walk back to our hotel."

"The next day, as we are packing up to go to *Le Havre* to take the boat back to the United States, we had accumulated so much loot on the way back. As we were packing, the chambermaid came in. I said to myself, 'I know how to get rid of this stuff,' and beckoned to the chamber maid."

"I said to her, 'Sit down,' and she did."

"Dallas and I started loading her up with all the stuff we got from the Repo Depot, things like gum, toothpaste, and candy. And Jay yelled, 'Send her in here when you get finished!'"

"She sat there on the bed, and looked at us expectantly, and I could read her thoughts, 'What do I have to do to deserve all this stuff?'"

"I said, 'Parti! Parti!'"

"She stared at me unbelievingly, and I said, 'Go on! Go on!' So she left."

"As we arrived on the first floor and exited the elevator, she was standing against the wall, with all this loot clutched to her breast, and the manager is yelling at her. She sees us and pointed at us, saying something in French."

"I said, 'It's okay!'"

"The manager looked at us and had a look of amazement and disbelief on his face."

"Were there any surprises when you got back to the States?"

"Well, yeah, there was one really nice thing that happened. You see, I got sent to Miami Beach, Florida, for three weeks of rest and rehabilitation. Well, that was nice and all, but while I was at the train platform, waiting to board my train back to Fort Bragg, I ran into the soldier who suffered from frostbite, the one who wanted to die? That guy was on the platform! I spoke to him a little bit. Turns out that the Germans did right by him and took good care of him. He recovered quite well. That was a nice coincidence, I think."

"So how did being a POW change you, if at all?"

"I think that before I was captured, I was a pretty happy–go–lucky kind of guy. I was more concerned about myself than other people. But my experience over there I think did more to shape who I became as a man and a person than any other experience, of that, I have no doubt."

"How did it shape you?"

"Well, when you are suddenly focused on things like life, liberty, and getting enough to eat, the values that you develop from this experience are far more important than anything you've done or had happen to you before. I personally thank God that I was a POW because ninety–percent of the Forward Observers who started in the war were killed during the war. If it wasn't for my capture, I doubt I'd be talking to you today."

"I learned to value the things in life that are really important... family, friends, and a reliance on God. My friends commented on the change in my personality after I came back, and I realized that my experience made me appreciate life so much more than I had ever done so in the past. So I'm grateful for the experience. Don't get me wrong...I wouldn't give a nickel to go through it ever again but I wouldn't trade a million dollars for what I learned through that experience. It changed me forever."

"When you came back, you arrived by boat. I'm curious: what was it like to see the Statue of Liberty?" the Emmett asked.

"Oh gosh, it was so very important. It means so much to me. That statue stands for so much: life, liberty, freedom, and home. All of us were thrilled to see that Statue of Liberty."

"In looking back over your entire prisoner experience, is there something that you realize now, that impressed upon you the most? That meant the most to you?"

"Well...given that there were so many chances and opportunities for something to go wrong, for the three of us to wind up dead because we chose to go left rather than right, or that we could have been captured because we made a simple but fatefully bad decision, I would have to say that in the end, I was certain – and still am to this day –That God must have had some of his angels watching over us. Someone," Frank pointed up with an index finger, "Someone up there was looking over us. Without a doubt. We couldn't have made it otherwise."

Author's Note:

When I first met the man who would become Frank Battle in this tale, I immediately saw that this was a man who, above all, deserves respect. Bob Corbin is a real leader, in the truest sense of the word. He is a former CEO of a business and a 24–year State Legislator of the Ohio State House of Representatives, so he knows about leading people. He expects to be listened to and obeyed.

Why? You might ask.

Because he has lived, as you have seen in this tale, through hell and back. He understands the worst of man and also the heights that a man can aspire to. He comes from a different age, a different world that I slowly have begun to understand and respect.

Bob Corbin comes from a time where you said what you meant, meant what you said, followed through on commitments, stood up when no one else would stand up to what was wrong. He comes from an age where you respected others because that's what you should do, not for how much money they had or what they could give you in return. He comes from a time where tradition and standards and morals meant something.

I would encourage each and everyone of you who read this book, if you are not a veteran of World War Two, then seek one out, ask them questions, get their stories.

Why?

Because they are a dying generation.

They're almost gone.

Don't miss the veritable treasure you might have living down the street, apartment complex, or hallway. You might learn something about history. You might learn something about the world. You might learn something about yourself and who you can really be.

That is one thing that Bob has taught me.

Even I can be a hero, if I persevere in what is right, true, and just.

Philippians 4:8–9

Finally, brothers, whatever is true, whatever is honorable, whatever is just, whatever is pure, whatever is lovely, whatever is commendable, if there is any excellence, if there is anything worthy of praise, think about these things. What you have learned and received and heard and seen in me– practice these things, and the God of peace will be with you.

Alexander Doyle
April 5, 2010
February 28, 2011

CPSIA information can be obtained at www.ICGtesting.com
264096BV00001B/2/P